This book belongs to:

....

....

....

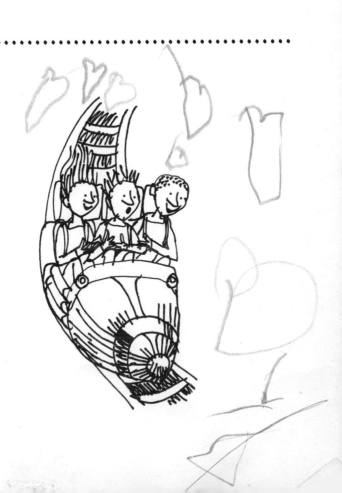

Stories for 9 Year Olds

Written by Nicola Baxter,
Moira Butterfield,
Nick Ellsworth, Marcel Feigel,
Jan and Tony Payne

Illustrated by Tim Archbold
(Graham-Cameron Illustration)

Designed by Blue Sunflower Creative

This is a Parragon book
This edition published in 2006

Parragon
Queen Street House
4 Queen Street
Bath BA1 1HE, UK

ISBN 1-40544-725-7
Printed in England

Stories

for

9

Year Olds

p

Contents

The Haunting of Holler Hall

Willoughby Junction is a small, quiet sort of village. If you don't live there, you've probably never even heard of it. There are two places in *Willoughby Junction* that everyone tries very hard to avoid. One is the dentist's surgery. The other is Holler Hall. Its real name is Hollow Hall. It was named after the rather misty and miserable hollow in the ground where someone in the 17th century decided to build it. But everyone in Willoughby Junction calls it Holler Hall. You would find out why they call it Holler Hall if you happened to walk past it on a moonlit night. You would hear things that would make your hair stand on end. It is said to be the most haunted house in the land. And its ghosts are very, very noisy.

No one ever wanted to go near the place. No one had been there since the last Lord Willoughby fell into the well. Local people guessed that the house was almost a ruin now. But they wouldn't have dreamed of cutting their way through the thick weeds and bushes to find out. As old Mrs Mabbs said to Ernest Bugg one day, shaking her walking stick, "There's no need to go looking for trouble. It'll find you soon enough."

It was good advice, but there was something about old Mrs Mabbs that always made people want to do exactly the opposite of what she said. The way she shook her stick didn't help. Mrs Mabbs lived in the middle of Willoughby Junction, so she could keep an eye on everyone, and on everything they did. Mrs Mabbs liked to know what her neighbours were doing, however boring it was. She knew when Mr Jones popped out to get the morning papers. She knew when Sarah Brooks fell off her bike and bumped her bottom. She knew when Jimmy Crisp went fishing instead of going to school (and she told his teacher about it).

Ernest Bugg wasn't the only person in Willoughby Junction to find Mrs Mabbs annoying. But he was the only person to do something silly just because she told him not to. He had never been very interested in Holler Hall. Not until he heard the old lady warning him and his friends not to set foot there. There and then, the great idea grew in young Bugg's mind. He would visit the haunted house and show everyone (especially Mrs Mabbs) that he wasn't scared of a few stupid old ghosts.

Now, Ernest Bugg was sometimes silly

(and this was one of those times) but he wasn't completely crazy. He decided that his first visit to the old house would not be at midnight, when the wind was howling and dark, ragged clouds covered the moon. He would make his first trip there in daylight, on a hot summer afternoon. And he would take a picnic with him.

On the first hot, sunny day, Ernest packed himself a large picnic of cheese-and-pickle sandwiches and chocolate cake. He put it in his rucksack, pulled on his walking shoes and set off for the lane that led to Holler Hall. He was looking forward to his walk and his picnic.

And he had just a tiny feeling of bravery that made the afternoon even more perfect.

As Ernest walked along the main street of Willoughby Junction, lots of curtains twitched. Curtains were always twitching in Willoughby Junction. It was that kind of place. But no curtain twitched more often than Mrs Mabbs's. When she saw Ernest, she even rapped loudly on the window with her stick. Ernest found at just that moment that he had a terrible need to cough. And his coughing didn't stop until he was out of sight of Mrs Mabbs's house.

As Ernest strolled down the lane, birds sang in the hedges and cows munched happily on the lush, green grass. It seemed impossible that there could be any kind of spookiness in such sunny weather. After half an hour he stopped and had a long drink of lemonade. Tramping along with a heavy rucksack was hot work.

At last, Ernest saw the narrow farm track that led to Holler Hall. He turned off the lane and walked down the track towards the hollow. He couldn't see the deserted mansion, but he knew that it was hidden among the trees and brambles up ahead.

There were lots of tall, leafy trees on both sides of the track. Their branches hung down, making it shady and cool for Ernest as he walked along. In the leafy shade, only the odd splash of sunlight lit the way ahead. At first it was easy to walk along. But the further he went, the narrower the track became. Soon it was little more than a path. Trees crowded in on every side. Soon Ernest had to work hard to push through the branches that blocked his way. Twigs snatched at his rucksack. He wished that he had brought a stick to beat his way along the path. In fact, he thought, Mrs Mabbs's walking stick would have been perfect.

As Ernest Bugg went on, things did not get any better. In fact, they got a lot worse. Nettles stung his ankles, even through his socks. Thorns scratched his arms and caught in his hair. Once, he stumbled on a root and fell head over heels into brambles and bracken. His cheek hit the damp, cold earth with a slap. When he looked up, he got his first shock. A small, mud-coloured toad was watching him from a mossy stone. For the first – but not, I'm afraid, the last – time, Ernest shuddered.

The Buggs are determined people and Ernest did not think of giving up. The path was slowly winding downwards into the famous hollow, so he knew he was almost there. He didn't want to turn round and scramble back through the thick brambles and branches. So he carried on stumbling down towards the hollow.

The path became so difficult that Ernest was almost crying. He was stung and scratched all over. He was afraid that he might get stuck or have to go back. Then, all of a sudden, he stumbled into a clearing. High above him, he could see the walls of Holler Hall at last.

Ernest felt smug. He had made it this far. Nothing really dreadful had happened to him yet. But he did need a little cheering up after his journey along the old farm track. Cheese-and-pickle sandwiches and chocolate cake seemed just the right thing. He sat down in the shadow of the wall and opened his rucksack. He was looking forward to a well-earned lunch.

It was at this moment that the first shriek rang through the air around Holler Hall. The shriek was Ernest Bugg's. There were more than a hundred little wiggly worms in his rucksack. They were slowly squirming their way out of his packed lunch. And the fat little worms showed every sign of having eaten rather well. Ernest threw the packed lunch away from him with the shriek I mentioned earlier.

Ernest's shriek had contained some horror. He really did not like worms very much at all. He heard his own yell fading into the afternoon. But then a second scream rang through the air. It wasn't Ernest this time, and it was much, much worse than Ernest's scream. He was frightened out of his wits as the sound echoed around the building behind him.

Maybe that was not the most glorious moment in the life of a Bugg. Ernest crouched on the ground and – the truth must be told – wailed in fear. Several more screams shook the peace of the quiet afternoon.

At last Ernest stopped wailing. He was now too scared to make any noise at all. After a short while, the horrible screams stopped too. He waited until everything was quiet once more.

Crouching on the ground is not a very dignified position for a heroic ghost-hunter. After a few minutes, Ernest began to feel a little bit silly. Slowly, he raised his head and looked around him. He peered left and right, up and down. But he could see nothing strange or ghostly. He could only see the dark branches stretching towards him and the towering walls of the house. More to the point, there was nothing to be heard, either. The only sounds were the thudding of his own heart and the not-very-pleasant noise made by one hundred worms squiggling back into the soil.

Ernest picked himself up and brushed himself down. He left his lunch where he had thrown it and gave his rucksack a good shake to get rid of any worms left inside. Then he began to walk around the walls of Holler Hall to find a way in.

You may think he was foolish. You may think he was brave. As a matter of fact, Ernest was neither. But the Buggs are well known for being very stubborn people, and Ernest was no exception. He had decided that he wanted to explore Holler Hall. So that was exactly what he was going to do, no matter what.

Ernest gritted his teeth and crept around the corner of the building. Straight ahead of him was one of the grand entrances to the hall. Swallowing hard, Ernest walked up to the entrance. It sounded very much as if someone else was creeping along just behind him. But he pretended that he couldn't hear a thing. Once or twice, he looked quickly over his shoulder. But he never saw anyone.

Ernest stood at the doorway and looked inside. The wooden door was falling to bits, and it was hanging off its hinges. The roof of the building had fallen in long ago. But there were lots of trees around the walls. Their branches and leaves hung over the building like a kind of roof. They made it very gloomy inside. Ernest wished he had brought a torch, but who thinks about torches on a bright, sunny afternoon in summer? Anyway, it was too late to turn back now. He walked slowly past the door and into the crumbling old entrance hall.

No one had cleaned this place for years, thought Ernest. Roof tiles, twigs and the skeletons of lots of small animals all crunched under his feet. He had to work hard just to keep his balance. *Crunch. Crunch.* Suddenly Ernest thought he saw something move, high up on the walls. He froze. But his footsteps didn't. *Crunch. Crunch.* Ernest Bugg looked down at his feet to make quite sure they were not moving. They weren't. An uncomfortable feeling squiggled down his back. He waited. There was no sound. He took a single step. *Crunch.* He waited. *Crunch.* There it was! Ernest was sure now. There were a lot of footsteps crunching through Holler Hall that afternoon. But only half of them belonged to him. What he had to worry about now was who the other half belonged to.

When you are halfway across a room with tiles and twigs and skeletons on the floor, you cannot move without making some kind of sound. It was very scary for Ernest Bugg to go on, but he had no choice. He tried to stop counting the crunches, but his mind seemed to do it anyway. Several times, Ernest took a deep breath, gathered all his courage and spun around. But there was no one there.

There was another doorway at the opposite end of the entrance hall. When Ernest looked through it, he could see that the rest of the house looked even gloomier. To make things worse, Ernest started to smell something very strange. It was not a very nice smell. A tiny thought about what very old, very dead bodies smelt like flitted into his mind. But Ernest was a Bugg. He gulped and went on.

Ernest crunched through the second doorway and saw a long corridor stretching out in front of him. He took a deep breath and started walking down the dark passage. Roof tiles were piled all over the floor and he couldn't help knocking them down as he went past. They made a very loud clattering sound. Ernest thought that there was much more clattering going on than one pair of feet could make. But it was not as scary as the crunching had been. Ernest walked quickly over to the next doorway. The door was half open. Ernest slowly peered in.

He was surprised to see a huge room that was clean and tidy. Someone had been sweeping up. The white marble floor was spotless and shining. In the far corner

Ernest could see a big, round hole in the floor. He knew that it must be the famous well, where the last Lord Willoughby had died. There was an enormous pile of plain brown cardboard boxes in the middle of the room. Ernest hurried over to take a look. The boxes had no writing on them to tell him what was inside. But one of the boxes, high on the pile, was open at the top. Ernest was just standing on tiptoe to look inside when he heard something that made him freeze in terror.

"Stop right there, young Bugg!" cried a voice that he knew very well. Before Ernest could say anything, he heard a ghostly voice repeat the words. "Stop right there, young Bugg!" It was an echo! Ernest almost laughed out loud. How silly he had been! All that shrieking and all that crunching had just been echoes! Holler Hall wasn't haunted at all! There was nothing here to worry anyone, except...

"So you thought you'd put your nosy little beak into my private business, did you?" hissed Mrs Mabbs. "The Mabbs have been having trouble with the Buggs since time began, but it stops right here. You can't say I didn't warn you."

Ernest turned around slowly. Mrs Mabbs was standing in the doorway and glaring at him. She was shaking her stick too. Ernest Bugg looked at the old woman. She had annoyed and scared him all his life, but she was much less scary than the things he had been imagining. He couldn't help smiling to himself.

"So what is all this, Mrs Mabbs?" he asked. "I can see it's something you don't want the rest of us to know about."

"Let's just say that it's a little business of mine that isn't quite legal," said the old woman. "There was no need for you to come poking your nose into everything. Holler Hall has been good to me over the years. No one bothers me here. The echoes have helped me to make Holler Hall one of the most haunted places in the country!"

"So it was you, all the time!" gasped Ernest. Mrs Mabbs cackled happily.

"Of course, there aren't really any ghosts here," she told him. "I just do a little bit of screaming on moonlit nights every now and then. Most people are cowards, and they stay away. But you Buggs always cause trouble. So now there is going to be another terrible accident here. What a shame that no one covered the old well after the last Lord Willoughby fell into it. Everyone in the village will hear how poor, curious young Ernest Bugg came out here all by himself, tripped over and fell into the open well. How very sad."

And the old woman cackled again.

"Don't be silly," said Ernest. "How are you going to make me jump into a well? I'm much bigger and stronger than you are."

"Like this!" cried Mrs Mabbs. She gave a screech that echoed loudly through the ancient house. As she danced towards him, Ernest saw something that made his blood freeze. There was a shining blade at the end of her walking stick. It was a sword stick! The shafts of sunlight coming through the broken roof made the blade glint and shine. Ernest backed away. Now he knew that the old woman was crazy. There was no telling what she would do.

As he backed away from Mrs Mabbs, Ernest kept thinking about the deep, deep well in the ground behind him. He took a quick look over his shoulder. The dark rim of the well was only a few steps behind him, sunk into the marble floor. Three more steps…two more…one more …he was going to fall in!

Suddenly, Ernest felt a pair of strong arms lifting him right off the floor. He found himself hovering above the well. With a yell of rage, Mrs Mabbs ran forward. Then she seemed to trip over something. She gave a terrible scream as she staggered towards the deep well. With a yell of fear, she fell.

Her screams filled the building and echoed all around. They grew fainter as she fell further down the well. Then, at last, there was silence. Ernest felt himself being put back down on the ground. His mouth was very dry. But he turned to thank the person who had rescued him just in time.

"My pleasure," said the last Lord Willoughby.

He raised his hand in farewell and walked away...through the ancient wall of his haunted home.

Grandma's Secret

It was raining at Grandma's. She said it was coming in off the sea, which was only a street or two away from her cottage. Ellie and Jack didn't mind going to Grandma's for their holidays, but when it rained it did sometimes get a little bit boring.

Grandma never seemed to be bored, and she didn't mind bad weather.

"It's just a shower," she'd say, and she'd put on a white plastic rain hat and a big red waterproof coat that covered her up almost completely, except for a pair of black boots that peeked out at the bottom. Then she'd march off into town with her old black-and-white dog Cyril on his lead, trailing the children behind her. Grandma always carried a cane with a silver shell mounted on the top. She was never without her cane.

Every day Grandma walked through town, sometimes to get her hair done in the tiny pink hairdresser's shop on the seafront, sometimes to buy some vegetables or a newspaper, and sometimes just to talk to other ladies she knew. In the grocer's shop she had a tiny birdlike friend named Beryl, who always called Jack and Ellie "poppets". She wore a curly silver shell, like the one on Grandma's cane, on a chain around her neck. Another of Grandma's buddies was a very large lady called Flo, who was to be found squeezed behind the counter of the newsagent's. She had a curly silver shell on a brooch.

Every day, come rain or shine, Grandma would take Cyril down to the seafront for some exercise and the children would go, too. They would hunt for shells.

"Try to find the curly ones," Grandma would say. "They're the best, though they're the hardest to spot."

Cyril's main enemy was next door's ginger tomcat. The children didn't know his name but Grandma called him "that evil creature". Often he sat staring at the cottage for hours, hunched under a bush, until Grandma chased him away with a broom. The cat sometimes tried to get into the cottage, too, but he never succeeded because Cyril would usually spot him coming and chase him away.

The other thing Grandma did was go to meetings. She never explained what they were about, but Ellie and Jack guessed they were to do with town litter or summer fairs. When Grandma was out, Mrs Liddle would babysit the children. She always brought her knitting and always fell asleep in front of the TV.

Today, Grandma had gone to a meeting, taking Cyril with her. The rain pitter-pattered against the cottage windows and Mrs Liddle was snoring softly in the armchair. There was nothing for Jack and Ellie to do. They couldn't play 'catch' or anything lively in the cottage because every shelf was crammed with ornaments. There were statues, vases, decorated boxes and paperweights with real flowers trapped inside them.

"Which is your favourite thing in the whole of Grandma's house?" Ellie asked.

"Guess," Jack replied. "And I'll guess yours."

But that wasn't very hard. They both knew which was the best, the most amazing, of Grandma's treasures. It was a model ship inside a bottle. It sat on the windowsill halfway up the stairs, looking out towards the sea. It was an old-fashioned ship, with sails made from stiff paper and lots of tiny threads for rigging. The name *The Windhorse* was painted on the side in gold letters, and there were tiny figures frozen in action on the deck. By the ship's wheel, there was a captain wearing a black three-cornered hat.

This ship in a bottle was the only ornament that Grandma had asked the children never to touch. But on that fateful day, as they sat on the stairs admiring the boat, something happened that was quick and shocking. The ginger tomcat from next door leapt out of an upstairs room. He launched himself down the stairs towards them, his eyes glowing like coals and a screech tearing out of his throat.

"Oh!" Ellie cried and bumped into Jack, who swayed forwards and knocked the bottle. It slipped off the shelf and smashed onto the floor.

Between one breath and another, the floor and the walls of the cottage seemed to vanish. Jack and Ellie sped through darkness, like passengers on a rollercoaster that had gone out of control. Then they slithered onto something smooth. As soon as they touched it, they saw daylight and water spray slapped across their cheeks.

Ellie and Jack were no longer in Grandma's cottage. They were on an old-fashioned ship with sails and rigging. There were sailors busy on the deck, and behind the ship's wheel stood a captain with a black three-cornered hat.

"Onward, boys! Catch the wind!"

roared the captain as the ship plunged through the waves.

Ellie clung to her brother.

"Are you in my dream?" she cried.

"I don't know. Are you in mine?" Jack gasped in return.

Two gnarled hands grabbed them both firmly by their shoulders. A giant of a man with cracked reddened skin and a rag tied around his head had taken hold of the two children.

"Stowaways!" he shouted. He lifted them off their feet and carried them to the captain.

"So, we have a couple of little thieves on board, do we?" the captain hissed.

"We're not thieves!" Ellie cried. The captain curled his lip.

"We're all thieves on this boat, and if you're not then you don't belong, and we'll drop you over the side. Won't we, Grittles?

Shall we feed 'em to the sharks?"

This last question was directed at a ginger cat who sat at his elbow. It stared spitefully at the startled children.

The captain came close to them. His nose was purple and his teeth were stained a dirty yellow.

"Why are you here?" he demanded.

"We...we...just liked your ship," Jack stuttered.

"Is that so?" said the captain. "You came aboard *The Windhorse* when we were in harbour, did you?"

The cat miaowed and the captain picked it up. He seemed to listen to the cat as if it were speaking to him. Whatever he heard, his face clouded with rage.

"So, you are Whitemane's brats! Throw 'em down below!" he ordered.

With their hands tied, the children were taken below decks to a small cabin with a window of bars in its rotting wooden door.

"Did you hear what the captain said? We're actually on *The Windhorse*, the boat from Grandma's house," Ellie whimpered, bewildered.

"And the captain's cat looks just like the one from next door," Jack added. There was a knock on the bars and a man with a stomach as round as a rum barrel grinned toothlessly at them. He pushed some crumbling mouldy bread through the bars.

"The captain sent this to keep your hunger from gnawing out your innards," he rasped.

"Please, what does the captain mean when he calls us Whitemane's brats?" Jack pleaded.

The man tapped his swollen nose with his finger.

"If you want to survive past suppertime, you'd better call him by his name. He's Captain Toolley, and don't you forget it. He's a black-hearted pirate. If you're Whitemane's spies, you'll be sorry."

"But who is Whitemane? We have no idea!" Ellie cried desperately.

"A cursed pirate-hunter, and Toolley's greatest enemy, that's who," the pirate hissed.

He pulled away from the bars, and looked around nervously as if he'd said too much. Then he scuttled away, leaving behind a small flickering candle stub on a shelf in the passageway.

Ellie crept quietly over to the door. She slipped her tied hands between the bars in the door and reached out towards the candle. Then she held the rope over the flame until it turned brown and began to smell of burning. Quickly Ellie snatched her hands back and rubbed the rope on the jagged wood of the door edge. The rope began to fray and split where it had been weakened by the flame.

Soon Ellie was able to free her hands.

"Well done!" Jack whispered.

"What do we do now?" Ellie asked as she untied Jack.

"We need more information," Jack replied.

They heard someone clattering along the passageway outside the door. It was the fat man coming back to collect his candle.

"How are you doing in there? Are you seasick yet?" he chuckled.

Jack waited until the man was outside the cabin door, turning away from them to pick up his candle. At just the right moment, Jack shoved his shoulder against the door as hard as he could. The rotten door broke open and slammed into the man's back. He toppled over, and the children leapt out, sat on him and pinned his arms behind him.

"Tell us where this ship is going," Jack threatened.

"Say you were the most powerful pirate on the seas, but someone is out to put a stop to your crimes. You'd want to defeat that enemy forever, wouldn't you?" hissed the pirate bitterly. "'Twas only a few weeks ago that we met Whitemane in battle and had to retreat. We've been in harbour since, having repairs, and now we're going to get our revenge."

"Where is Whitemane's hideout?" Jack asked.

The man dropped his voice: "That was once a secret to all but Whitemane's crew. But now Captain Toolley has had information from a spy."

There was a soft hiss behind them. Grittles, the ginger cat, was crouching in the shadows arching its back.

"I didn't tell!" the man croaked, plainly terrified. The cat put out a claw, as if to scratch him. Then it leapt up the ladder and disappeared above.

"You may as well give up, little devils.

He's gone to warn them," the man muttered. Sure enough, other pirates soon came rushing along the passageway to grab the children once more. They were taken on deck to Captain Toolley.

"I shan't let you out of my sight again, devils. You will help me get my revenge, very soon," he growled.

"Land ahoy!" came a cry from up in the rigging. An island appeared on the horizon. The crew lowered several rowing boats and the children were lifted down into one of them.

"We need to keep you safe. You're precious," Captain Toolley grinned nastily as they swept towards the shore. He was the first to step on land, carrying Grittles the cat under his arm.

"Whitemane is close," he hissed. "I will soon show her who is the strongest and most cunning between us."

"Did he say HER?" Ellie muttered to an equally surprised Jack.

The captain dropped Grittles, then led them along a narrow path that snaked through thick jungle.

"That cat is a spy," Jack remarked under his breath, but the captain heard and cackled.

"That's right, little devils. Grittles knows all about Whitemane's lair. Oh yes. And he knows about you, too. He has been watching Whitemane very carefully."

"Toolley," a voice suddenly rang out through the jungle trees.

Captain Toolley started wildly. His skin seemed to lose its colour.

"Whitemane, I have your brats," he cried out.

Captain Toolley shoved the children forward into a jungle clearing, where an extraordinary sight met their eyes. Boxes of treasure were piled around. Sitting among them were several pirates...and every one a woman. A particularly small birdlike pirate woman nodded towards the children.

"All right, my poppets?" she asked.

"It's Beryl, from the grocer's!" Jack gasped.

A very large lady pirate pulled out a gleaming sword from her belt, and Captain Toolley's crew flinched.

"It's Flo from the newsagent's! This is too weird!" Ellie declared.

The Queen of the Pirates sat on the biggest treasure box. She had white hair that escaped in curls from under a white scarf. She wore a magnificent long red coat, black boots and carried a cane with a silver shell on the top. A black-and-white dog sat by her side, growling softly.

"Whitemane," Captain Toolley hissed.

"Grandma!" the children gasped.

"Who was it who told you the way to my secret lair, I wonder?" Grandma murmured. Her gaze flicked from Captain Toolley to Grittles the cat. "Who was it who helped to release you from your imprisonment and capture my grandchildren? An evil pirate cat, that's who!"

"Grandma..." Jack began.

"Hello, dears. You'll be wanting to ask what Cyril and I are doing here," she said. Then she leaned towards them. "When I was younger I discovered there was a way through to another world. I found it full of wicked cruel pirates, and the worst one of all was the evil Captain Toolley. It took me a long time, but I gradually gathered a good crew around me, and eventually I caught him and his gang of cut-throats. Only his black-hearted cat escaped." Grandma pointed angrily at Grittles.

"Surrender, Whitemane!" Toolley screamed. "Or your brats will suffer!"

"Has Grittles not told you about my magic?" she murmured.

The captain took a step back and looked confused.

"Grittles, what is this?' he whispered urgently.

The cat yowled, as if making some complaint or perhaps an excuse.

"What do you mean, you were never able to discover her magic? What magic?" The captain furrowed his brow, seeming not to understand.

"The last time we met it was 20 years

ago, Toolley," Grandma said quietly. "I used my magic to catch you and your crew. But you don't remember. You have no memory of those two lost decades, I don't suppose, and that's a blessing for you. I turned you all into wooden men and trapped you in a bottle, to rot with your ship. Only your cat escaped."

"No! You are mad!" Toolley shouted. "We fought you only weeks ago. *The Windhorse* has been in harbour since then!" He passed his hand over his brow. He seemed not to know, or not to remember, what had really happened to him.

"*The Windhorse* sat enchanted on my windowsill for 20 years. Then Grittles found a way to make my grandchildren break the bottle, and it tumbled back into the pirate sea with them on board."

"You lie! We have been in harbour!" the captain screamed. He pulled out his

sword and held it over the
children.

Grandma shook her
head, almost as if she
pitied him.

"You can't win, Toolley,"
she murmured. Then she
waved her cane as a signal,
and pirate women swarmed
in from the surrounding
trees. They were all from
Grandma's town. There
was Grandma's hairdresser and all her
assistants, the lady from the Chinese take-
away and the women's bowls team who
normally played on the seafront. Each of
them had a curly silver shell in her hand.

When the treacherous pirate cat
Grittles saw them all, he screeched and
leaped into the undergrowth. As Captain
Toolley swung his sword Grandma lifted up

her cane. She put her mouth to the curly silver shell on the top of it and she blew. The other pirates put their own shells to their lips, and blew at the same time.

There was a sound like waves crashing on the shore, mixed with a ship's bell. The rollercoaster feeling returned. The children sped back through darkness, only this time accompanied by a blood-curdling scream from Captain Toolley. They blinked, and found themselves back in Grandma's cottage with the babysitter Mrs Liddle, who opened her eyes and sat up in her armchair as if nothing had happened.

"Your grandma will be home soon. I'll put the kettle on," she murmured, and shuffled out of the room, just as Grandma appeared in the doorway with Cyril on his lead.

"I want to show you something," Grandma smiled.

The Windhorse was back on the windowsill, trapped in its bottle. Captain Toolley stood, tiny and frozen, at the wheel. His crew stood immobile on the decks.

"When I first came across Captain Toolley he was far too strong for me to beat," Grandma remarked. "I had only one magic shell back then. I'd found it on the beach and when I blew into it I found I could travel between worlds. Every day after that Cyril and I went back to the beach, until we gradually found more and more shells. We had them covered in silver for safety, and gave them to our friends to help us. In the end, we found that when we blew into all the shells together, our magic was too strong for Toolley. We turned *The Windhorse* into wood, along with the captain and his crew, and trapped them all in the bottle. Only Grittles escaped. He's been trying to save his master ever since."

"He sat staring at your house..." Ellie murmured.

"That's right, dear. He found a way back to our world, by hiding in someone's handbag or coat pocket, I dare say. Then he watched and waited for his moment."

"I broke the bottle," admitted Jack guiltily. "I'm sorry, Grandma."

"Never mind. It's turned out right now," Grandma smiled and cuddled them both.

Grittles never returned to Grandma's cottage. When the children came back for another holiday, *The Windhorse* had disappeared from the windowsill. Grandma had given it to the local museum, because she thought it might be safer there.

Holidays at Grandma's were much more exciting after that. She gave each of the children a magic shell, and when she went 'off to meetings' she always took them with her.

Martha Makes a Mistake

L ily was having her portrait painted.

"Smile," said her brother Jake, sucking the end of his paintbrush as he concentrated on the picture he was trying to do for his homework.

"I can't smile. I'm thinking," said Lily.

"You think all the time. You think for the world!" Jake remarked. It was true. Lily was a deep thinker who liked to work things out carefully and quietly in her head. Jake was more of an 'action first, think later' kind of guy. He scribbled quickly on his picture.

"There! What do you think?" he cried, holding it up for Lily to see.

Lily's face remained solemn. There

was a long pause. "Well?" asked Jake.

"Oh...er...sorry. I was thinking of something else. Is it finished?" Lily asked.

"Yes! Well...I'm bored with doing it now," Jake grinned.

"Hmm...I think I like it!" Lily announced and laughed.

"Good! Then let's go down to the beach to find some shells!" Jake cried. He bounced up, ready to do something new.

Lily and Jake lived in a small village on the coast. Their house was five minutes from the sea and nearly every day they walked on the beach with their dog Charlie. Their seashore was very beautiful, with cloud-washed skies and blue-grey sea. There were brightly coloured fishing boats and beach huts dotting the shoreline.

The children felt happy when they got home from their walk, but their mood soon changed. They heard the phone ring, then mum's voice rising and falling.

"Who was that?" Lily asked when Mum came back into the kitchen.

"It was my old friend Martha," Mum said. "She's coming to stay for a week."

"A week!" Jake exclaimed.

"And she's bringing her nephew Simon," Mum added.

Jake and Lily glanced worriedly at each other. Martha was a very old friend of Mum's, and she had been to stay a few times before. She complained about everything and was very fussy and bossy. She didn't like dogs, and said they spread germs and hairs and had smelly breath. Whenever she came, Charlie would go and hide because she told him off such a lot.

"Do you remember what that battle-axe said last time she stayed?" Jake whispered to Lily. He imitated Martha's voice: "Animals sleeping on beds isn't

hygienic." He shook his
head in disgust. "She
doesn't know
what she's on
about. Charlie is
always licking
himself, so he
must be clean."

"Come on, she's not
that bad," Mum said. "She's just not used to
children or dogs."

"I wonder what Simon's like," Lily said.

"You'll find out soon. He's going to
share Jake's bedroom," Mum replied.

"That's not fair! He might be horrible,"
Jake complained.

"What about putting up the tent in the
garden?" suggested Lily.

"Good idea," said Mum. "The
weather's fine. You can all camp out. It will
be an adventure."

"Hmm," Jake grunted doubtfully. "I don't suppose Martha will let Charlie sleep in the tent."

Jake was right about that. "Oh, Simon loves camping, don't you, Simon?" Martha declared when she arrived with her nephew and heard what was planned. Simon himself didn't get the chance to say anything as Martha continued: "Simon won't mind roughing it, but you won't let that dreadful dog in, will you?"

Simon looked as if he was about to say something, but his aunt didn't stop to listen.

"I can't stand dogs. I'm sure Simon feels the same," she declared. Jake scowled. He didn't like the sound of Simon.

That night in the tent the children tried to chat to Simon, but he was very quiet. He snuggled deep inside his sleeping bag and they thought he had gone to sleep.

"He's really stuck up!" Jake whispered

to Lily.

"He's probably shy," Lily whispered back, and she turned off the torch they had taken to the tent.

Suddenly Simon sat up, and made them both jump.

"Can you leave the torch on?" he asked. He sounded really upset.

"The batteries will run out," said Jake.

"It's pitch black without it," Simon cried.

"The house is close," said Lily, "and there's a light on in the kitchen."

Simon went quiet for a minute, then he cried out again.

"Can you hear footsteps?" he asked.

"No," said Lily.

"You've got the torch," said Simon. "Can you go and look? I can't sleep until I know there's no one out there."

This went on all night. Strange noises,

strange voices, thunder and lighting...you name it, Simon heard it. When morning came the children had hardly slept at all.

"I'm sure Simon loved the tent. You should do it again tonight," Martha suggested.

"I think we should sleep in my room tonight," Jake told his mother quietly, when Martha wasn't around. "I think Simon was really afraid of the dark."

That day the children were going pony trekking.

"Simon will ride brilliantly, I'm sure," said Martha when they were all eating breakfast in the kitchen.

Simon looked absolutely miserable.

"Do you like riding?" Lily asked him, but as usual his aunt didn't wait for him to answer. "He tried it once when he stayed with me before. I think it's such a good hobby to learn. I want Simon to have a proper mount, not some slow old pony for beginners."

"I'm sure they'll find him something suitable," said Mum.

"I hope so," said Martha. "Otherwise it will be so, so boring for Simon."

"Simon, Simon, Simon!" Jake whispered to Lily, annoyed. "She makes it sound as if he can do anything!"

When they got to the riding school, Lily saddled up Raffles. She had been riding him for a year and they were great friends. Raffles was calm, intelligent and willing. In fact, his personality was very similar to Lily's. They were a good match.

Jake had a sweet little pony called Max. He was a bit naughty sometimes, but lots of fun and he got on with Jake perfectly.

Martha had persuaded the riding instructor that Simon was a very experienced rider.

"I don't want some old nag who can't even gallop," she insisted, as if she was going to ride it herself. Simon was given a pony called Buster. Lily knew that Buster could be a bit of a handful. She warned Simon, who looked absolutely terrified.

Once they started it was clear that poor Simon wasn't the expert rider that Martha had made out. He bumped up and down in the saddle and he tugged and pulled at the bridle until Buster's mouth was sore. Eventually Buster had had enough. He dug in his heels and stopped suddenly. Simon was catapulted over his head and landed in a heap on the ground.

"Are you all right?" Jake cried.

"Stupid pony!" Simon muttered unhappily and began to cry.

"It's OK, Simon. We've all fallen off before," Lily reassured him. "I get the feeling you don't really like riding. Am I right?"

Simon nodded miserably.

"I tried to tell my auntie, but..." he sniffed.

"She doesn't listen...I noticed," Lily nodded. "Simon's pony must have been startled by something," she told the riding instructor when they got back. "He's all right now," she added quickly.

"Well, I shan't let him ride there again," Martha declared angrily. "The ponies obviously aren't trained properly."

That night the children slept in the house. Simon shared Jake's room.

"Can we keep the light on?" Simon asked before they went to bed, but Martha overheard him.

"Don't be silly, Simon," she snapped. Jake was beginning to feel really sorry for Simon, because Martha just didn't seem to take any notice of how he felt.

"Are you a little bit scared of the dark?" he asked Simon, once they were in bed.

"Yes...but not just a little bit," Simon whispered. "I tried to tell my auntie but she just told me not to be so childish."

Jake put the bedside lamp on for Simon. Then they chatted before they went to sleep.

"Is that your picture?" Simon asked, pointing at Jake's portrait of Lily.

"Yes. Rubbish, isn't it!" Jake laughed. Simon asked if he could borrow some paper and pencils, and drew a really brilliant picture of Jake sitting up in bed.

"Wow! You're a really good artist!" Jake cried when he saw it.

The next morning Jake showed it to Lily.

"Simon's great at drawing. But when I said I was going to show it to Martha, he told me not to bother. He said she wasn't really interested in what he liked doing, only what she thought he should like." Jake told his sister.

"Hmm..." Lily began and then went quiet.

"You're going to do some thinking, aren't you? I can always tell, because you say 'Hmm' and then you stop talking," Jake grinned.

That day a picnic was planned on the beach. It was a lovely warm sunny day.

Mum owned one of the small brightly painted beach huts in the sand dunes.

"I thought it would be nice if we had our picnic and then just lazed around swimming and sunbathing," Mum suggested, and that sounded so good that even Martha agreed.

"Is it OK if we take our art stuff? We thought we could do some pictures on the beach," Lily asked Mum.

"That's a great idea," Mum agreed.

The picnic was just right. There was cold chicken and salad and crisps and some of Mum's delicious home-made pie. This was followed by meringues, and strawberries and cream. It was perfect. Even Martha seemed to enjoy it, but she had noticed a funfair back on the seafront and, instead of swimming and sunbathing, she insisted they go to see it.

"There's a big dipper. Simon will love

that. The bigger, the better, isn't that right, Simon?"

Simon went quite white and didn't answer.

"She's such a bully," Jake hissed. "She's like an evil auntie from a fairytale!"

"I think Simon stays quiet because he doesn't want her snapping at him," Lily replied. "He ought to tell her how he feels. Then she might be less bossy. I've got a plan to try to change things but we need to get back to the beach..."

Then she told Jake about her idea.

The fairground was fun. It was noisy and crowded. The most noise came from the big dipper. The children stood eating candyfloss and watching the little cars snake to the top of the big ride, then pause before whooshing down the other side at terrific speed. The screams from the children and parents were deafening.

"I expect you two would like a go," said Mum.

"Of course they would," said Martha. "And Simon. I've already bought you tickets."

Lily looked at Simon. His face was flushed a dull red.

"You don't have to go on it," she whispered.

"Yes, I do," he muttered unhappily. "And I hate heights."

"Don't worry. We'll help you," Jake told him quietly. "Get in the car with us."

"Simon, don't you want your own car?" Martha demanded, as he stepped into the car with Jake and Lily, but it was too late for her to boss him around. The ride operator put the barrier down, pressed a button, and away they went.

"I'm going to hate this!" Simon wailed.

"Shut your eyes, and remember that

we're here with you," Lily reassured him. She and Jake held onto his arms so he felt safe.

"Ooooooooh!" cried Simon as their car climbed a steep slope and then plunged down the other side. People screamed all around them, and so did Simon. But it sounded more like a scream of excitement than one of fear.

"With my eyes closed, this is really fun!" he cried, as the car climbed once more to the steepest part of the ride.

"Get ready," grinned Jake. "Whoooooaaaaa!"

They raced down the drop on the other side. Then the ride was over and the car trundled towards the exit.

"Thanks for helping me," Simon told Lily and Jake.

"No problem," said Jake.

"Anyway, you were the brave one, going up there when you are scared of heights," Lily added. "Does it feel good to be a hero?"

"Yes, it does!" Simon laughed, for the first time on his visit.

They all went back to the beach, planning to laze around. But Martha had a different idea.

"I want to do a cliff-top walk," she insisted. "Come on now, Simon. You'll enjoy this."

"We want Simon to do some art with us," Lily interrupted.

"Yes, he's fantastic at art," Jake added.

"Nonsense. Simon, come on." Martha turned to go.

"N...no...I'd rather do the art," Simon piped up. His aunt looked as if she was about to tell him off for not doing what he was told. Then Mum saved the day.

"I'll go with you, Martha. We'll be able to see the children from the path. Before Martha could disagree, Mum grabbed her by the arm and drew her away.

"Well done for standing up to that old bossy-boots," Jake grinned, when the adults were out of hearing range.

"I think it would be a good idea to tell her how you feel about things," Lily suggested. "I'm sure she's not all that bad. She's just got into the habit of telling people what to do and not listening to them."

They unpacked their art paper and coloured pencils.

"I'm going to draw the sea," Lily said.

"I'm going to draw a whale and a shark in the water!" Jake declared.

"Hmm..." Simon muttered, and wandered off up the beach, carrying his art things. They drew happily for a while. Jake was the first to give up, and he went to the water's edge to skim some pebbles and see how many times he could make them bounce over the surface before they sank.

Lily carefully drew the waves lapping on the shore and added some shells scattered along the beach. Then she drew Jake throwing a stone. When she had finished, she saw Martha and Mum waving from the cliff path.

She went over to where Simon was busy drawing, alongside a fishing boat pulled up on the sand.

"I think they're coming back," she warned him, then looked at his picture.

"That's amazing, Simon!" she gasped.

When Martha and Mum returned they were keen to see the children's pictures.

When Martha saw Simon's drawing her mouth fell open, and then she said:

"Well!"

"Simon, you're a wonderful artist," Mum smiled. "Martha, you must be proud. You didn't tell me your nephew was so talented."

"Er, no..." Martha replied. "To tell the truth, I didn't know. Simon, you should have told me before."

"I did try..." Simon replied, "...and I'm afraid of heights, and the dark," he blurted out. His aunt looked stunned and was silent for a moment. Then she took his hand.

"Oh dear! Simon, I haven't been a very good aunt, have I? I've been telling you to do this and that, and not asking you what you really want," she sighed.

"That's okay," Simon replied. "Look, I've named the boat after you." He had written the word 'Martha' on the side of the boat he had drawn.

"I reckon your thinking worked," Jake whispered to Lily. "Perhaps Martha will think twice before bossing Simon around in future."

"I'd like to think so," Lily grinned.

Swimming
with
Dolphins

"Wow! Look at that," said Sam excitedly, pressing his nose against the car's back window. It was his first view of the sea, from high up on the mountain road. Sam and his parents had been coming to the same island every summer, ever since he could remember. They always stayed in the same house, and Sam always got this first fantastic view of the sea as they drove to it from the airport.

As soon as the car had crunched its way up the small lane that led to the house, Sam jumped out, happily feeling the hot sun hitting him full in the face.

"Can I go swimming, Mum?" he asked.

"If you give me a minute to unlock the

house and get changed into my swimming cozzy, I'll come with you," replied Mum, easing herself out of the hot, sticky car.

"I suppose that leaves me to carry the cases in," groaned Dad, mopping the sweat from his face.

"Looks like it!" said Mum with a laugh.

She unlocked the front door, then she and Sam got changed quickly, grabbed a couple of towels and ran out of the back door and down the steep steps that led to the sea.

"Race you there, Mum!" Sam yelled, running towards the water.

"Ow. It's hot!" shouted Mum as her feet touched the sand.

"Run faster. Then it won't hurt!" Sam yelled back as he dived into the waves.

The sea rushed over his body, cooling him off instantly. He heard his mother splash in behind him.

"Ah, that's better," she said, swimming up to him. "The best way to cool off."

After they were too tired to swim any more, Sam and his mum sat on their towels on the beach looking out at the great sheet of water in front of them.

"It looks like it goes on forever, doesn't it?" said Sam, gazing into the distance.

He saw something glinting in the water, far out at sea.

"Hey, what's that?" he said, shielding his eyes from the glare of the sun.

"Maybe it's a boat or something," said Mum.

"I don't think so," said Sam, screwing up his eyes even tighter.

Whatever it was, it seemed to be darting around in the water very quickly, but at the same time moving steadily across the horizon.

"I know what it is!" he yelled excitedly.

"Dolphins! There must be at least 30 of them. Look at them, Mum! They're leaping in and out of the water!"

Mum stood up to get a better look.

"How wonderful," she said. "In all the years we've been coming here, I've never seen anything like this before."

They both watched silently, until the dolphins were out of sight.

By this time, the sun had started to sink and the heat of the day was over, so they decided to gather up their towels and make their way back to the house.

"Oh, there you are," said Dad, watching them climb the last of the steps into the garden. "I hope you two realize that I've not only got all the luggage in, but I've unpacked it and put it away as well."

"Sorry, Dad," said

Sam, hanging his head a bit. "But Mum and I saw something so incredible, we just had to stay and watch."

"And what was that?" asked Dad, with a grin. "Me lugging in all the cases, I suppose."

"I'll tell you later," Sam laughed.

After he and Mum had showered and changed, they all met on the balcony and decided to go out to their favourite island restaurant, 'Ocean'. Sam liked it a lot, because it had the best pizza he'd ever tasted in his life.

They got into the car and drove up the coast road, higher and higher until they reached the very top.

'Ocean' stood right on the edge of the cliffs, and Sam had often wondered why it hadn't crashed into the sea on very windy nights. But the little restaurant hadn't, and here it was, all lit up, as inviting as ever.

"Ah, Sam and family!" said a voice at the door. "How nice to see you all again. Please come in."

The voice belonged to the head waiter, Dominic, who had been there for years.

"Nice to see you too, Dominic," said Dad, giving him a hug.

"For my old friends, the best table in the house!" said Dominic, and he led them through the busy restaurant to the balcony outside. The air was cooler out there and, although it was too dark to see the sea, you could hear it crashing onto the rocks far below.

"My goodness Sam, you've grown so much since I saw you last!" said Dominic, brushing down the tablecloth with his napkin.

"Well, I'm a year older than last year," said Sam.

"This is true. How stupid I am!" said

Dominic, pulling out a chair for Sam's mum.

'Ocean' served the best pizza on the island, so that's what they always ordered when they went there.

"Pizza, please," they all said. Sam's mum chose a vegetarian one, Dad had a seafood one, while Sam went for his usual, a pepperoni with extra cheese topping.

After ordering their food, Sam told Dad about the dolphins he and Mum had seen earlier.

"I've never seen anything like it in my entire life!" said Sam enthusiastically. "They were leaping out of the water and criss-crossing each other as they went along. It was incredible, wasn't it Mum?"

Mum nodded in agreement and was about to say something when Dominic arrived with their food.

"Thanks, Dominic. This looks delicious," said Dad.

"May I sit down? I have something interesting to tell you."

"Of course," said Dad, pulling up a chair.

"I heard young Sam and his talk of the dolphins," said Dominic excitedly. "Indeed, it is a beautiful thing to see, yes? But, I have something even better. Sam, how would you like to go swimming with the dolphins?"

"Swim with them? But how?" asked Sam in utter astonishment.

"My cousin," continued Dominic, "he has a boat and he has a secret call."

"A secret call?" asked Sam, a little confused.

"Yes, a whistle, a

special whistle that can bring the dolphins to him. This is very secret, you must not tell this to anybody!"

"I won't!" said Sam.

"I believe you, Sam," said Dominic kindly. "Now, listen carefully. I will ask my cousin, his name is Armando, to take you on his boat, where he will whistle for the dolphins to come. Then, when they come, you can swim with them."

"Swim with them?" asked Sam, hardly able to believe his ears.

"Yes, swim with them."

Sam was so stunned, he didn't know what to say.

Later that evening, Dominic phoned them at the house to say that he had already spoken to Armando who would be happy to take Sam to the dolphins the very next day. Sam was so excited he hardly slept a wink that night.

The next morning, they piled into the car and drove down to the little white fishing village where Armando kept his boat. Dominic was already there, and waved to them.

"Over here, everybody!" he shouted. "Here I am!"

Next to him stood Armando. He was slightly taller, but much younger with a big mop of curly black hair and a huge grin on his face. After everyone had said hello, Armando turned to Sam.

"So, Sam. You come out with me in my little boat today, yes? Today, you swim with the dolphins?"

"Yes, please," replied Sam.

"Yes, please! You are a very polite boy, yes? I like that. It is good to be polite, yes? Come on. I show you boat."

They all trooped aboard Armando's boat, which was docked a few steps away.

It wasn't very big, but Armando kept it sparkling clean. It was painted red and white and had a small cabin that was just big enough to seat two people.

"It's lovely!" said Sam's mum.

"She is lovely, yes," said Armando. "She is called 'Dom', in honour of my favourite cousin, Dominic, yes?"

Dominic blushed wildly, but was clearly very pleased to have Armando's boat named after him.

"You'll look after Sam, won't you," asked Mum a little nervously.

"Not to worry," replied Armando. "He is very safe with me. I am with him all the time, yes? We will be back before the sun goes down."

"Armando knows this sea like the back of his hand," said Dominic. "And look at the sea! It is as flat as a pancake."

It was time to go. Sam waved goodbye

to his family as the little boat chugged out to sea. Armando was whistling happily at the helm. Sam took a good look around. The sea was so calm it looked as if they were travelling across a flat desert. A desert of blue water.

Armando threw him a life jacket.

"Put this on," he commanded.

"But I'm the best swimmer in my class," protested Sam.

"I have promised your mother that you wear it. You can take it off when you swim with the dolphins."

Lying on the small deck with the

chugging of the boat in his ears and a gentle sea breeze fanning his face, Sam almost fell asleep. At last, Armando's voice brought him wide awake.

"OK, Sam, we here now, yes? Help me to drop the anchor, please."

Armando and Sam dragged the heavy anchor to the side of the boat, and then heaved it into the water.

"What happens now?" asked Sam.

"Now, we whistle for the dolphins."

Armando put his thumbs together and blew thinly through the gap between them. A strange noise came out, halfway between a whistle and the hoot of an owl.

"Look easy, yes? In fact, is very difficult. You try." said Armando.

Sam copied Armando exactly but, when he blew, no sound came out at all.

"I tell you is difficult," laughed Armando and, putting his thumbs together, he made the strange sound again.

Sam's eyes searched the sea, but there was no sign of any dolphins.

"Look!" cried Armando, pointing. "Here they come. Come on, my dears. Armando is here with friend Sam, to say hello."

Sam couldn't believe his eyes. On the horizon, heading straight for the boat, was a small school of dolphins. There were about 12 of them, and they were leaping through the water and criss-crossing each other, just as they had been when he saw them with his mum on the beach.

"Wow!" cried Sam.

"Indeed, wow," laughed Armando. "Now, Sam, look at this. Now I show you something."

Armando quickly got a bucket full of small fish. As the dolphins reached the boat he grabbed a fish, holding it tightly in his outstretched hand. One of the dolphins flew high out of the water, grabbed the fish in his mouth in mid-air, then disappeared into the water again.

"Fantastic!" said Sam.

"Indeed, fantastic," chuckled Armando. "Now you try."

Sam took a fish from the bucket, walked to the edge of the deck, and then nervously held it out in front of him. Before he knew what had happened, a dolphin had leaped out of the water and taken the fish out of his hands, then disappeared over the other side of the boat.

"I didn't feel a thing!" exclaimed Sam excitedly.

"The dolphin is most gentle creature. He will never hurt anyone," said Armando softly. "Now Sam, is time you have been waiting for. Is time to swim with the dolphins."

"Are you coming in too?" asked Sam anxiously.

"No, no, there is no need. They will treat you like baby," smiled Armando.

Sam pulled off his life jacket, took a deep breath and jumped into the clear, cool water.

When he surfaced he realized that he was surrounded by the dolphins. They swam very close, softly nudging him with their heads. Sam knew at once that they were only playing and gently pushed them away with his hands.

"Hold on to the big one's fin!" yelled Armando from the deck. "You will get wonderful ride."

Sam did as he

was told and suddenly found himself being whisked through the water at high speed, holding on to the fin with both hands as tight as he could. The dolphin leaped through the air, then dived just below the surface so Sam didn't go under too. The other dolphins swam close by, as if trying to catch them. It was the most amazing game of chase Sam had ever known. He swam and played with the dolphins for a long time, until finally he heard Armando's voice from the boat.

"Sam! You must come aboard now. The wind, it is getting up. We must go back now."

Sam climbed aboard as Armando started the engine and turned the boat around. The boy looked back at the dolphins who had begun to swim in the opposite direction. As usual, they were leaping through the water, making their strange squealing sounds as they went. It was as if they were saying goodbye to him.

"You have good time, yes?" asked Armando at the helm.

"The best day of my life," replied Sam. "Please teach me the whistle to call them. I promise I won't tell anyone else."

Armando thought for a moment.

"OK, Sam. You are good boy. I do this for you."

Armando sat on the deck and showed Sam the exact position the thumbs should be in, and the exact pressure Sam should blow through them with his lips. After half an hour and many failed attempts, Sam finally blew through his thumbs and out came the perfect whistle.

"Brilliant! Now you can do it. Remember, this is just for you." warned Armando.

By now, the wind was stronger, it had

started to rain and the waves were getting much higher. The little boat began to rock from side to side. Sam started to feel scared.

"It's OK," shouted Armando above the howl of the wind. "I am best sailor in village. I get you back safe, no problem."

Just then, the engine spluttered, and without any warning it stopped altogether.

Sam looked at Armando, but he was already making his way down the steps to the engine compartment, spanner in hand. Suddenly, he slipped on one of the wet stairs, and landed with a heavy thump on his back.

"Armando, Armando!" yelled Sam, rushing up to him.

But Armando was out cold and, with a sickening feeling in his stomach, Sam realized that he was completely on his own on a stormy sea, on a boat without an engine. To make matters worse, water was now sloshing over the sides of the boat quite quickly. He grabbed a bucket and started to bail the water out. But as fast as he could bail it out, the water was coming in twice as quickly. He knelt by Armando's unconscious body, pleading with him to wake up.

"Wake up, Armando. Please wake up. The boat's sinking and I don't know what to do!" But Armando lay still.

Suddenly, Sam had an idea. The dolphins would help him! He put his thumbs together and blew through them.

No sound came out. He wiped his hands and tried again. This time it worked. The whistle came out long and low, cutting through the noise of the wind and rain. Again and again he whistled. Then he heard a noise. At first he thought it was the wind, but then realized that it was the dolphins' calling sound. And there they were, 30 or 40 of them, bounding through the waves towards him. They surrounded the boat and began to nudge it along, using their heads.

Sam was so relieved, he wanted to cry. The dolphins pushed the little boat for many hours until the storm had passed, and the sky was clear.

Up on the deck, Sam had tried to make Armando as comfortable as possible. Suddenly, Armando moaned and sat up.

"Ow! My head. What happened?" he groaned, rubbing it.

"You were knocked unconscious in the storm and we were sinking, so I whistled for the dolphins and they saved us!" said Sam breathlessly.

Armando stood up slowly and saw that the dolphins were still tirelessly pushing the boat.

"Incredible!" he shouted. "In all my years, I never see anything like this. It is a good thing I teach you the whistle, yes?"

Armando leaned down to the dolphins. "Thank you, my friends. I fix the engine well now. You can rest."

The dolphins stopped pushing, slowly turned around, and then joyfully leaped through the waves back out to sea.

"Thank you, my friends! You saved my life!" yelled Sam, waving furiously at them.

Not long after, the engine roared into life.

"We will be back very soon now," said

Armando at the wheel. "Well, young Sam. What a day you have had, eh? I think you will remember this day all your life, yes?"

But Sam wasn't listening. He was watching the last of the dolphins flying like a bird through the water, its majestic fin glinting in the dying rays of the sinking sun.

I Kissed a Frog

Prince Tarquin George Louis DeBeer of Margrovia was heir to the throne of his beautiful country. Added to that, he was young, good looking and very popular, which only made a certain rotten relative hate him more. Unknown to Tarquin, his Uncle Roland was determined to get his hands on the crown of Margrovia.

Roland made it his business to know every hidden secret of royal life. He poked around in the vaults below the Royal Palace, where all sorts of antiques and treasures were stored. There, he found something long forgotten.

"This is my chance!" he hissed and

immediately went to find his nephew, Prince Tarquin.

'Tarkers', as his friends sometimes called him, was in the library arranging his latest polo and sailing trophies. Uncle Roland slithered up behind him.

"Tarquin, dear boy, I see you've won yet more prizes. How clever you are," Roland remarked. "But the palace is getting so cluttered, don't you think? I've just been down in the vaults to see if we can find some more room."

"Oh, right," Tarquin replied, uninterested.

"Yes...and it's quite extraordinary what bits and pieces are down there," Uncle Roland continued. "One item...in Vault 13...well..." He leaned closer to Tarquin and spoke more quietly. "I think it's something very strange and powerful!"

"What exactly are you talking about,

Uncle?" Tarquin replied, startled.

"I can't say more. I've already revealed too much. I forgot there are certain things you are not supposed to be told, my boy. For your own good, of course. I do apologize. Please forget I ever spoke of Vault 13!"

Uncle Roland fled, his bony hands held up to his face in fake horror.

"What does the old duffer mean? Are there secrets being kept from me? That's not fair! Where is Vault 13 anyway?" Tarquin muttered.

Being a young man of action he immediately went to investigate the palace vaults. Down there it was like a mad junkshop. There were vases, paintings, carvings and sculptures, all labelled with the name of the country they came from and the date they were collected by some royal person or another. Tarquin moved through the vaults, counting them until he reached number 13.

Vault 13 was almost empty except for a small wooden box on a table. Tarquin stepped forward and flipped open the lid. Inside he saw a plain grey stone about the size of a tennis ball. The inside of the box lid was engraved:

If you are a prince, be warned,
Those who touch the stone are scorned.
They must face their hardest quest,
To find the kiss of a true princess.
With her kiss they will be free...

Just as Tarquin was about to read the

next line there was a noise behind him. His Uncle Roland stepped forward from the shadows and pushed him towards the table. He toppled over, knocking the stone out of the box and accidentally brushing it with his hand.

Immediately he felt different. For a start, everything around him suddenly seemed huge. The table towered above him and the ceiling of the vault looked as far away as clouds in the sky. His hands felt odd, too. He looked down and was horrified to see that they had turned green. His fingers had grown long and a piece of thin green skin stretched between each one.

Uncle Roland, now giant-sized, knelt down beside him and chuckled. He held a small mirror in front of Tarquin, who stared at his reflection in frozen horror. A small green frog stared back at him.

"Aaargh!" croaked Tarquin.

"It won't do to have frogs in the palace. I believe it is my duty to kill this one immediately," Roland remarked.

"Kill? You've gone crazy!" Tarquin gasped. He leapt over his uncle's foot as it swung towards him and hopped as fast as he could towards the stairs.

"Come out, Tarquin, my boy. I was only joking about killing you," Roland wheedled, but his murderous voice said otherwise.

At the far end of the vaults the stairs now looked impossibly high for a frog. But they were Tarquin's only escape route, so he began to hop up one step at a time.

At last he reached the top and skidded around a corner, to come face to face with Winston, the palace cat. Tarquin was only saved from certain death because Winston was fed snacks all day by royal butlers and had grown very fat. He couldn't move as fast as Tarquin, who leapt up onto a suit of armour displayed in the corridor. It crashed over, sending him flying out through an open window.

Tarquin fell through a drain grate in the palace courtyard and landed inside a dark, smelly drainpipe. When he hopped out of the end he found himself, shaken and confused, in the cool green public park outside the palace.

Tarquin was a brave young man and tried never to give up when things got tough, but it was hard going struggling through the park's long grass.

"There's a worm over there. Mmm. It might be tasty," he muttered to himself, then felt shocked when he realized what he'd said. "I can't believe it! I want to eat worms!"

He struggled on, but then got tangled up with a discarded sticky sweet paper that fixed itself to one of his legs.

"Get off!" he cried, but every time he shook his leg the paper tangled further around his foot. He bumped his head on a park bench and, when he looked up he saw a pair of blue eyes staring down at him.

"Hi," he said, as calmly as he could. "I don't suppose you could...er...help me with this sweet paper, could you?"

The eyes belonged to a young lady who opened her mouth and shut it like a fish, in silent surprise.

"Oh, I'm being rude not introducing myself. I'm Prince Tarquin," he blundered on. "You've probably seen me in that magazine you're reading."

The girl had a copy of *Famous!* on

her knee. It was the kind of magazine that is filled with photos of celebrities in their lovely homes and members of royal families on holiday or shopping. Tarquin hopped up onto the bench, startling the girl. She drew back from him, gripping her magazine.

"Don't be frightened, please," Tarquin begged. "What's your name?"

"Alice," the girl replied suspiciously.

"Er, well then, Alice. I'm in a spot of bother with this sweet wrapper. Could you, er...?"

He tried to smile, though he wasn't sure whether frogs could. They can't. He just ended up looking crazy. But Alice was one of those rare humans who just wants to help others. So she gingerly put out her fingers and yanked the wrapper off his foot.

"Thank you! What a relief!" Tarquin cried.

At this point Alice stood up hurriedly.

"I've obviously had too much sun and I'm dreaming. Frogs don't talk. Jamie! Jamie! We're going!" she called out to a boy who was playing on the grass nearby.

"No, no! You can't go! Let me explain!" Tarquin cried. He made a desperate lunge and grabbed the back of Alice's T-shirt, screaming, "I am Prince Tarquin, heir to the throne!"

Alice ran towards the boy as Tarquin clung on for dear life, shouting madly.

The boy came over and stared down at Tarquin.

"Aunt Alice...you've got a frog on you," he said.

"Please, please help me!" Tarquin whimpered.

"Cool! The frog talks!" Jamie remarked, and gently picked up Tarquin in his cupped hands.

"Who are you? What do you want?"

Alice demanded.

"I am Prince Tarquin. I have been turned into a frog and I need to kiss a princess," Tarquin replied, trying and failing to sound casual.

Alice looked at him suspiciously, then turned to a photograph in *Famous!* magazine, showing Prince Tarquin on the ski slopes with some other people. She glanced at the photo, then at the frog, then back at the photo.

"OK, if you're really Prince Tarquin you'll be able to name these other people in the picture," she said. She showed him the photograph, with her hand over the caption.

"Certainly I can," Tarquin replied confidently. "That blonde with the horsey face is the Honourable Lavinia Stottbuttle. The man with three chins standing next to her is Julian St Cloud Walajinsky De Vere, and the woman with the unbelievably silly hairdo is his third wife, Lady Caroline."

"You ARE Prince Tarquin!" Jamie cried, delighted that his holiday had just got a million times more exciting.

Alice and Jamie took Tarquin back to their hotel, where they switched on the TV news. Reporters were gathered outside the palace, where wicked Uncle Roland was filmed standing on the balcony, making a speech:

"Prince Tarquin has run away. We think he has gone mad. He has left a note saying he no longer wishes to rule Margrovia," Roland announced. "Unless he reappears in 48 hours, I will become your new king."

Tarquin was outraged to hear such lies about him. He swelled up alarmingly.

"Are you going to burst?" Alice gasped.

"Wait until I get back to normal! I'll imprison my uncle in a dungeon!" Tarquin cried.

"To get back to normal you have to be kissed by a royal princess, right?" Jamie asked.

"Yes, according to the inscription on the box," Tarquin said.

Jamie began to leaf through Alice's copy of *Famous!* magazine. "Here's one," he pointed to a picture and read out the caption: "Monardo's royal beauty Princess Marie is seen at a charity fashion show with Baron Humbert Torkenstein. Friends of the couple say that marriage is in the air."

"What rubbish," Tarquin scoffed.

"Humbert is a bore. Marie can't stand him. She told me so at the last inter-royal Christmas get-together. Her mother is trying to make Marie marry him because he has lots of money. Look, Marie is the only princess for miles around. She's my only chance, and the quickest way to Monardo is by plane. Please, please, please will you take me to the airport?"

It wasn't easy for Tarquin on the plane to Monardo. He was stuffed inside Jamie's pocket along with a packet of chewing gum, some coins and an unpleasant-looking handkerchief. Every time Jamie wriggled in his seat, all the stuff in the pocket moved around, including Tarquin, who tried desperately to stay away from the hankie and ended up sitting painfully on a coin.

When they reached Monardo, they took a taxi to the Grand Hotel. That night a glittering party was held there. Everyone who was anyone had been invited, which meant that Alice, Jamie and Tarquin had not been asked.

They stood by the hotel entrance, watching a line of shiny black limousines arriving. In the largest one they saw Queen Primula, a thin woman with a nose that looked as if it had been pinched together by a peg. By her side was King Otto, a grim-looking man. They were hoping that by the end of the evening their youngest daughter, Princess Marie, would be engaged to the rich Baron Humbert Torkenstein.

Behind their limousine there were several others, including one carrying a very unhappy-looking Princess Marie.

"Quick! This is our chance!" Jamie cried. Alice knocked at the window of the princess's car.

"We need to speak to you! We're

friends of Tarquin!" she cried. Princess Marie quickly opened the door to let them inside.

"Driver, take us round the block," Princess Marie ordered, then looked eagerly at her new passengers.

"I heard that Tarquin had given up the throne! Is he all right?" she asked.

"Er, well. He's turned into an animal," Alice began.

"Isn't that typical! All men are animals!" Marie tossed her head.

"No, you don't understand..." Alice tried to interrupt but Marie had launched into a speech.

"Do you know Baron Humbert Torkenstein? Now there's an animal! He eats with his mouth open, and he picks his ear with his napkin. I can't stand him, but my mother insists I marry the oaf. I should run away like Tarquin." Marie's eyes widened with excitement.

"Not yet. We need you to kiss..." Alice tried again but Marie wasn't listening. She was pulling off her tiara and throwing down her rings and necklaces.

"Stop, driver! Stop! I'm leaving! I want to be a racing driver, not a princess! I'm going to do what Tarquin did. I'm going to follow my dreams!"

She wrenched open the car door and fled off into the night, before Jamie had even taken Tarquin out of his pocket.

The driver of the limousine turned to them.

"Do you want to go to the party?" he asked.

"No. You'd better make it the airport,"

Alice sighed.

"I'm doomed to lose the throne," Tarquin sniffed. "There are no more royal princesses for miles."

"We won't give up! What your uncle did is wrong and we are going to put it right," Alice insisted. "Our only hope is to get back into your palace. If you could touch the stone again, maybe you'd change back."

They took the next flight out of Monardo and reached Tarquin's old palace in darkness. There were lots of TV crews outside because time was running out for Tarquin. There was only one hour left before Uncle Roland would be proclaimed king.

"They won't let us in through the front entrance," Tarquin sighed, shaking his head sorrowfully.

"Excuse me. I'm a writer from *Famous!*

magazine," Alice cried loudly, pushing her way through the TV crews, followed by Jamie and a nervous Tarquin. People believed Alice and moved out of their way to let them reach the front door, but they ducked around the side of a pillar, where a small side door stood unlocked. It led down to the palace vaults.

They hurried straight to Vault 13.

Jamie set Tarquin down on the table and flipped open the lid of the wooden box. Alice began to read the inscription:

If you are a prince, be warned,
Those who touch the stone
are scorned.
They must face their hardest quest,
To find the kiss of a true princess.

"Stop right there," a nasty voice echoed behind them, belonging to none other than wicked Uncle Roland.

"I wondered if you'd come back at the last minute, so I took no chances," he hissed at Tarquin. He had an iron poker in his hand.

"It's time to finish you off good and proper," growled Roland, lifting the poker in the air. Jamie tried to grab Tarquin but Roland pushed him aside.

Alice snatched up the box.

"Tarquin! Listen to this!" she cried, and read the lines that Tarquin had missed the last time.

With her kiss they will be free...
A princess need not royal be.

'Tis one who proves she's true of heart,
Who with a kiss will play her part.

"Whoever kisses you doesn't have to be a royal!" Alice declared.

"Too late!" Uncle Roland shrieked and lunged towards Tarquin. Jamie stuck out his foot and tripped him over.

Tarquin leapt into the air and the poker missed him by millimetres! It smashed into the box, splintering the wood. The stone spun high into the air.

Tarquin jumped into Alice's arms.

"No!" Uncle Roland screamed.

"Yes!" Alice cried and planted a big kiss on Tarquin's froggy face.

Tarquin felt funny again, as if he were on a rollercoaster plunging downwards. Soon he was back to normal.

"You are true of heart, Alice. You saved me!" he cried.

There was a sudden shriek from Uncle Roland. He had put out a hand without thinking and caught the stone as it spun back down. Instantly he began to sprout hair all over his body. He shrank in size and a tail sprang out behind him.

"Yuk! He's turned into a dirty horrible rat!" Jamie cried, as Uncle Roland scuttled away.

"That will be a great improvement," Tarquin added.

The three friends went upstairs and Tarquin showed himself on the palace balcony. He decided that nobody would believe he'd been a frog, and they might think he really had gone mad if he tried to explain. So he told everyone he'd been locked in the vaults all this time by his wicked uncle, who had now run away.

In the next few months, *Famous!* magazine showed lots of photographs of Tarquin and Alice together. The magazine even suggested that the pair might get married. Who knows? You can't believe everything you read these days!

The Missing Mummy

Mrs Morris looked worried. There was a big frown on her forehead. She sighed three times as she tucked Millie and Max into bed.

"What's the matter, Mum?" asked Millie. "I'll clear up the mess in the bathroom tomorrow, honestly."

"It's not that, Millie," said her mother. "It's just that something is bothering me at work. I can't understand it at all."

Max hated to see his mum looking worried. He knew that her job as a cleaner at the museum meant a lot to her. She could only clean at nights, when the doors were shut to the public. Mrs Evans from next door always came in to sit with the children while she was out.

"Is it something we could help with?" asked Max. "We're good at solving mysteries. Remember how we found your watch for you at Christmas?"

Mrs Morris had lost her watch on Christmas Day. She was very upset because it had been a birthday present from the twins. Max and Millie had been reading a detective story, and they decided to find the watch. They worked out that it must be among all the wrapping paper from the presents. Sure enough, after half an hour of delving and diving and making a huge mess, Millie had spotted the watch at the bottom of the pile.

Mrs Morris smiled as she remembered.

"You're both great detectives," she said, "but this is a grown-up mystery. You see, no one is supposed to be in the museum at night, except me. But for the last week I've found that things have been moved *after* I've cleaned them but *before* I've gone home. That means there is someone else moving around the museum when I'm there. I've never seen anyone, but I know they must be there. Alf, the security guard, has never seen anyone either. I can't understand who it could be. There's no way anyone could get in without Alf seeing them."

"Isn't there any other way in?" asked Max.

"There is a loose window in the basement, but it's too small for a grown-up to squeeze through. What if something goes missing? I'm the only one with a key. I'm the only one that Alf sees going in and out. I'll get the blame if anything is stolen. And I can't afford to lose this job."

"You should tell the museum manager," said Millie. "At school, we

always have to tell the
headteacher if we see
something bad or
strange. You should
tell the manager
about things being
moved. Then they'll
know it's not you
if anything goes
missing."

Mrs Morris looked
a lot happier. She kissed
Millie on the forehead.

"You're absolutely right, Millie," she
said. "Clever girl! I'll pop into the museum
after I've dropped you both at school
tomorrow and see the manager. Now, lie
down, both of you. Mrs Evans will be here
any minute and I've got to go to work."

"You'll be careful, won't you, Mum?"
said Millie.

"If there's anything scary, hit it with your mop!" Max added.

"Goodnight!" laughed their mum. The twins went off to sleep. They felt sure everything would be OK once Mum had spoken to the museum manager.

But Mrs Morris didn't go to see the museum manager the next day, because she didn't come home that night. Mrs Evans waited until she was quite sure that something was wrong. She tried ringing the museum, but the phones were all switched off for the night. Then she rang the police. They promised to go round to the museum straight away to see what had happened.

Alf, the security guard, was sitting at his desk just inside the front door.

"We're looking for Mrs Mary Morris," the first police officer explained. "We understand that she works here."

"Oh yes, I know Mary," replied Alf

Gardner, "but you'll find her at home now. She left over an hour ago. Look, this is where she signed herself out in the book. Right here."

He handed the record book to the first officer, who looked at the place where Mrs Morris had signed her name.

"The writing looks pretty shaky to me," said the second police officer. "Was she OK when she left here?"

"Oh, she was in a hurry," said Alf. "She always likes to get back to her kids as soon as she can. But she does a good job, mind you. The old place has never looked as clean and well kept as it does these days. I can give you her address, if you like. I've got it here somewhere."

But the two officers just looked at each other and said goodnight to Alf. They already knew where Mrs Morris lived, and they knew that she wasn't at home. They walked through the dark streets, the way she would have walked home from the museum. But there was no sign of the missing woman at all.

Max knew that something was wrong as soon as he saw Mrs Evans getting breakfast in the kitchen next morning.

"What's going on?" he asked.

"Where's Mum?" cried Millie.

Mrs Evans decided that it was best to tell the truth.

"You mustn't worry, my dears," she said. "There's probably a very good reason why your mum hasn't come home. Maybe she stopped to help someone who was hurt. You know what she's like. And she hasn't been able to get to a phone to let us know."

"Mum would always let us know," said Max. "She would never stay out all night without letting us know she was fine. Something's happened to her and we need to speak to the police."

"I've already done that, dear," said Mrs Evans. "They're looking into it right now. They'll soon find her, I'm sure."

"No, I mean that Millie and I have some important information," said Max. "Mum told us something about the museum last night. I'm sure the police will want to 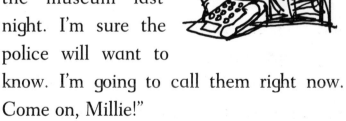 know. I'm going to call them right now. Come on, Millie!"

Max and Millie told the police all about their mother's worries. They explained about things being moved around at the museum.

"That's very interesting," Sergeant Fox

told them. "We'll go back to the museum straight away."

A couple of hours later, the police called at the house. Max and Millie were waiting for them.

"Have you found Mum?" asked Millie.

"I'm sorry, kids," said Sergeant Fox. "The security guard says he doesn't know anything about anyone breaking in at night. He says your mum never said anything about it to him. Do you think maybe she kept it to herself until she was sure?"

"Maybe," said Max, but Millie shook her head.

"No, I'm pretty sure she meant that she'd discussed it with Alf. He can't be telling the truth!"

"He's worked there for 20 years," said the first police officer, "and nothing's ever gone missing. I think he's pretty reliable. He's quite old and soon it will be time for him to retire. I don't think he'll do anything to put his pension in danger. Do you have any other ideas?"

Max and Millie looked at each other. They did have ideas, but they didn't want to tell the police about them just yet.

"Mrs Evans is going to stay with you until we find your mum," said the second officer. "Try not to worry. It's not easy to lose a whole grown-up person. We'll find her."

As soon as the police had left, Max and Millie went to sit in their tree house in the garden. It was high up in the oak tree, and they knew that no one could hear what they said.

"I don't like the sound of Alf," said Millie. "I'm sure Mum talked to him about it. If there was someone creeping around in the museum, then Alf isn't doing his job properly. Or maybe he's letting someone in.

And if there isn't anyone coming into the museum, then the person moving things around has got to be Alf himself. Either way, he's involved in this somehow."

"I agree," said Max, "and I think we should go over to the museum and have a look around. We can't find out anything staying here. And you know, Mum said we were good detectives. Let's slip out tonight."

Millie thought that was a good idea, so they made their plans. Now they just had to wait for bedtime.

Late that night, Mrs Evans put the twins to bed and told them for the 20th time not to worry. It was a silly thing to say, really. Of course they were worried. But they knew they would feel a whole lot better as soon as they started doing something about it.

It was easy to creep out without disturbing Mrs Evans. She had hardly slept

the night before and the
twins could hear her
snoring   gently.
They tiptoed down
the stairs and out
of the front door.

Max   and
Millie   hurried
through the empty
streets towards the
museum. If they saw
anyone coming, they hid in
a shop doorway. But it was late, and there
was hardly anyone around. At last they saw
the big doors of the museum ahead of
them.

Millie and Max peered through the
windows in the doors. They could see Alf,
the security guard, sitting at his desk in his
dark-blue uniform. He was reading a
newspaper and drinking a cup of coffee.

Behind him were lots of small television screens. They showed pictures of what was happening in all the rooms in the museum, from the security cameras.

"He's not even looking at the television screens," hissed Millie. "Anything could be going on in the museum and he'd never notice."

"Let's hope that's true," said Max. "Now, remember that loose basement window Mum told us about? Come on!"

Millie and Max crept around the corner and found the loose basement window. It was just big enough for them to squeeze through. Soon they were inside the museum. Some of the lights were still on, but it all seemed very dark and different at night. The twins had been there lots of times during the day, looking at interesting displays that their mum had talked about. But at night, when there were no other visitors around, it was a bit spooky.

"What should we do?" asked Millie. She was feeling very nervous.

Max looked worried, too.

"I'm not sure," he said. "I think we should just walk around and look out for anything that's out of place. We know these galleries well enough. We should notice. But we'll have to be careful to keep away from the cameras or Alf might spot us on one of his television screens."

"That's easy," said Millie. "They're in the same place in each room, and they are set for people a lot taller than us. If we work our way along the wall in each gallery, they won't be able to spot us."

"Then let's get going!" whispered Max. "I think we should stay together, don't you?"

"That's probably a good idea," said Millie, hoping she sounded as brave as Max did. She really didn't want to be on her own in this spooky building.

Everything seemed to be all right in the costume gallery. The models in their costumes and the suits of armour at the end looked a bit like ghosts in the dark. But they were all in the correct places.

It was the same in the Greek and Roman gallery. The vases, bowls and piles of coins stood silent and still.

"It all looks normal," whispered Max.

In the prehistoric gallery, the dinosaur skeletons and fossils looked the same as they always did. But, as soon as they entered the gallery of ancient Egypt, Millie stopped.

"There's definitely something different in here," she hissed. "Do you feel it?"

Max nodded. Something felt wrong, but what was it?

Very carefully, the children moved down the room, keeping close to the wall so the camera wouldn't see them. The stones covered in strange writing looked the same as always. The cabinets with jewellery, make-up boxes and little statues seemed fine, too. But, in the middle of the room, something was very wrong.

In the centre of the room there was a huge wooden box that had been found in an Egyptian tomb. It was decorated with gold, rubies and emeralds. On the lid of the box was a painting of a pharaoh, with his arms crossed in front of him. Many times when they visited the museum, Max and Millie had wondered if there was really a mummy inside the box.

Now they wondered even more, because the box was open. Its huge lid was on the floor and the twins could see inside at last. It was dark and empty, except for a single piece of bandage. Millie leaned forwards and picked it up.

"D-d-d-do you think there was something inside it?" Max asked.

"Y-y-y-you mean, something that's out here with us now?" replied Millie. "I don't know. I really wish I did."

"Anyway, this proves that there's something strange going on," said Max. He felt a little bit better now he knew that Millie was as scared as he was. "I'm sure this isn't meant to be open. But why hasn't Alf noticed? Isn't he supposed to walk around the museum once every hour, so that he can make sure everything is all right? How could he not have noticed this?"

Millie suddenly grabbed Max's arm

and made him jump.

"Sshhh!" she hissed. "I think I can hear him coming now! Let's hide behind this cabinet. Quick!"

They squeezed behind a tall display cabinet, and they were only just in time. Slow, thudding footsteps were coming down the gallery towards them. Millie peeped out from their hiding-place. Then she clamped her hand over her mouth so that she wouldn't scream.

"Is it Alf?" whispered Max.

"No!" Millie had never sounded so scared. Max peeped out and gasped. A huge mummy was walking down the gallery towards them. He was covered in ancient bandages from head to foot. There were dark holes where his eyes should have been. But, worst of all, he was heading straight for the twins' hiding place!

Millie and Max held on to each other.

They were trapped! There was nowhere to run to. Millie saw the huge shadow fall over them. Very, very slowly she looked up and stared straight into the mummy's terrible face.

But Max was looking at the mummy's feet, and he saw something amazing. A piece of dark-blue uniform was peeping out from under the bandages! Max knew something was wrong. He leaned forwards and grabbed a loose piece of bandage around the mummy's ankle. Then he pulled on it as hard as he could.

Max had only meant to see if the bandages came away, but he did much more than that. As he pulled on the end of the bandages, the mummy's feet slipped. It fell to the floor with a loud crash and banged its bandaged head on the display cabinet.

"Ow!" yelled the mummy.

"That didn't sound very Egyptian!" Max cried.

The twins thought fast. Millie raced forward and tied the loose bandage to the leg of a cabinet. Max did the same with the other leg and the two arms. There was no way that the mummy could move now. They had caught it!

"Now, let's find out what's going on," said Max. His face was very serious. He tugged at the bandages around the mummy's head and pulled them away. The twins saw a face they knew.

"Alf Gardner!" cried Max. "I knew it! What have you done with our mum?"

Alf groaned and spat.

"You nosy little brats! Why couldn't you

leave things alone? Your mother was just the same. Always asking questions and poking her nose in. I'll be retiring soon and my pension is tiny! I was going to take a few things I could sell. I want a bit of money in my old age. I should have known you two would be just like your mother."

"Where is she?" Max shouted. "What have you done with her?"

"Oh, she's fine," said the guard. "I would have been gone by tomorrow. Then you'd have found her, safe and well. She's shut up in the cupboard at the end of the prehistoric gallery."

Max and Millie ran back through the museum to the prehistoric gallery. They raced to the cupboard at the end.

"Mum! Mum!" yelled Millie.

Together the twins pulled the cupboard door open.

"Mmmmmfnnng!"

Inside, Mrs Morris was sitting on the floor. Her hands and feet were tied with rope, and there was a gag around her mouth to stop her from making a noise. Her eyes filled with tears when she saw her children.

"Oh, my dears," she cried, as Millie pulled the gag from her mouth. "I thought I'd never see you again. How worried you must have been!"

The twins were crying too. They were so happy that they couldn't speak.

"Hey, untie me!" laughed their mother. "How can I hug you when I'm tied up like this?"

Millie and Max untied Mrs Morris and she gave them both a big, long hug. Then they all went to telephone the police.

Sergeant Fox shook his head when he heard what Millie and Max had done, but he was impressed, too. So was the museum manager.

"It seems to me that you've got a lot to offer us," he told Mrs Morris. "Brains and bravery run in the family. How would you feel about becoming our Head of Security? There would be a big rise in pay, of course."

Mrs Morris could hardly believe it. She said "Yes" straight away!

"When could you start?" asked the manager.

"As soon as you like," smiled Mrs Morris. "With two great detectives like this to live up to, I'd better get some practice right away!"

The House on the Moor

"Mark, Tim, turn that light off. We've got an early start in the morning!" yelled Dad from the bottom of the stairs.

"OK, Dad," Mark shouted down from the bedroom. "We were just having a last check of our backpacks."

"You can check them in the morning. I'll wake you up at four o' clock. Goodnight, boys."

"All right. Goodnight," shouted Mark.

"Goodnight, Dad," shouted his younger brother, Tim. "See you in the morning."

Mark and Tim were excited. Tomorrow morning they were getting up bright and early to go on a whole day's hiking trip on

Ridlington Moor with their father. They'd gone on long afternoon walks with him many times before, but never one like this. Now that the boys were older, he felt that they were ready for a full day's hike.

The family had moved to the area only a few months ago, so Dad had never hiked on Ridlington Moor before. The boys joked with him that he was scared. Some people said that the moor had ghosts.

"Rubbish," he'd say. "I don't believe in ghosts."

It was still dark when they got up the next morning and finished checking their backpacks. They needed to take spare trousers and an extra fleece in case it got cold, as well as waterproof trousers in case it rained. Apart from the food and drinks that Mum had packed for them, that was all they took. The plan was to drive to the moor, lock up the car, then return to it in the evening.

"Bye, Mum," said the boys, giving her a kiss on the cheek.

"Bye, boys. Be careful, now. Look after your dad, won't you," she grinned.

"We promise!" laughed the boys, as they walked towards the car.

They put their backpacks into the boot, climbed into the car and drove off in the dark towards the moor.

After an hour, they'd reached the edge of the moor. By now it was daylight, and a crisp, bright, cool morning. It was perfect hiking weather. Dad and the boys put on their jackets, shouldered their backpacks, locked the car and walked out onto the springy purple heather.

It was still very early and they were completely alone. Ridlington Moor was one of the largest areas of moorland in the country. No one lived there and, as far as the boys knew, no one ever had. There were many ghost stories surrounding it that Dad had always laughed off. He had no time for ghosts and all that 'nonsense'. But the boys weren't so sure, and were glad that most of their hike would be during daylight.

Dad took his compass and map out of his pocket.

"Remember, boys, whatever else happens, we mustn't lose these. They will get us to where we want to go and back again without getting lost."

The boys nodded their heads in reply. Dad had always told them that a hiker without his map and compass was like a rowing boat without any oars. Going nowhere, fast.

"Right," said Dad, spreading out the map on the ground in front of them. "This is the plan. We're going to walk up to this small ridge of low hills here. We'll stop at the top and have something to eat. Then we'll make our way down to this small stream, cross over at the narrowest point, then continue around this valley until we reach the car again. I reckon we should hit the car as daylight's fading. Are we all agreed?"

"Sounds good to me, Dad," said Mark.

"And me," said Tim.

"Any time you want a rest, just tell me and we'll stop, OK?"

"OK," nodded the two boys.

As they walked, Mark and Tim enjoyed the smell of the wild flowers and seeing the surprised pheasants darting into the air ahead of them. After some time, Dad told them to take a break and eat something. Even after their huge breakfast, they hungrily tucked into their food.

"Don't eat too much, now," warned Dad through a mouthful of egg sandwich. "Remember, it's difficult to walk well on a full stomach."

When they had eaten, Dad consulted his map and compass. "If I'm right, we should be on top of the ridge in a couple of hours," he said.

The next two hours were going to be more difficult, as most of the way was uphill.

"Everyone all right? Want to stop?" Dad asked, after a while.

"How long to the top?" asked Tim, whose feet were hurting a little.

"Another ten minutes and we'll be there," said Dad. He was right, and ten minutes later they were standing on the top of the ridge, looking down at the windswept moor below them.

"Well done, boys!" he said. "That was a pretty difficult climb. You did really well."

Tim took a big gulp of water.

"Are you all right?" asked Mark, noticing his brother was hobbling.

"I'm fine," said Tim, not wanting to tell Mark how sore his feet felt. He took off his boots and rubbed his sore feet while Mark and Dad took out more sandwiches for lunch. The view was amazing. There was nothing for miles around, except for the empty moor. Tim felt a cold shiver run down his spine. It all felt a bit spooky.

After they'd rested and eaten, they set off towards the small stream over the other side of the ridge. Going downhill was, of course, a lot easier than going up. The boys started to chat together and Dad even told a joke, which meant he must have been in a good mood. He never told jokes usually!

As they got nearer to the stream, Tim's feet began to hurt again. Very soon, he started to hobble.

"Let's have a look at your feet," said Dad, noticing that his youngest son was falling behind. He gently eased off Tim's boots and thick socks.

"Hmm…they're not too bad," he said. "Just a little swollen. We'll be at the stream soon and you can give them a good long bathe in the water."

When they reached the stream, Tim bathed his sore feet in the cold water.

Suddenly, Dad started to search his pockets frantically. "I can't find the map and compass!" he said. He looked carefully through his pockets and backpack, but couldn't find them anywhere. Mark and Tim searched through their things too, but after half an hour of searching they realized that the precious map and compass were lost.

"I must have dropped them somewhere," said Dad, worriedly. "We'd better retrace our steps to the top of the ridge and hope we find them."

"But what about Tim's feet?" asked Mark.

"That's true," replied Dad. "He should rest them for a bit longer yet. We've a lot more walking ahead of us."

"I'll stay here and look after him," said Mark.

"I don't like the idea of leaving you two

alone," Dad said.

"Don't worry," replied Mark. "We'll be fine, and anyway, we're not likely to get into trouble with Tim's feet stuck in the water like this."

"That's true," Dad laughed.

"Go on, Dad," urged Tim. "We'll be fine by ourselves." Dad thought for a moment.

"All right," he said finally. "Don't move from here and I'll be back as quick as I can." He started to walk back up the hill.

The boys watched him go. They suddenly felt alone and a little nervous.

"Do you think there are ghosts on the moor?" asked Tim.

"Don't be silly," Mark replied. "Dad's right. There's no such thing as ghosts."

"I hope not," said Tim, looking around, almost expecting to see one.

By the time Dad returned, the sun was

getting low in the sky.

"Sorry, boys," he said. "I've looked everywhere. I just can't find them."

"What do we do now?" asked Tim.

"Well, I know the general direction of the car is that way," said Dad, pointing his finger towards the setting sun. "But it's a good three hours' walk away. Come on, let's make a start."

The boys gathered their things and followed their father across the moor. Tim's feet felt a lot better, so he easily kept up.

An hour later, they stopped to rest. Dad thought that they were walking the right way. But before very long the sun would go down, and they would be in more serious trouble.

All too soon, the last of the sun's rays disappeared behind a ridge of small hills. It was getting darker by the minute.

"Torches out, boys," said Dad.

Their three torches shone like small searchlights in the night. But they lit up only a few yards in front of them. The going was slow, and it was getting colder.

"Stop! I can hear something," said Dad, all of a sudden.

"Is it a ghost?" asked Tim, nervously.

"Don't be silly," whispered Mark. "Sshh…let Dad listen."

They soon realized that the noise was the tinkling of the stream that they'd rested at earlier.

"I can't believe it," cried Dad, shining his torch around him. "We've walked around in a great big circle!" Then, to make matters worse, it started to rain. Huge drops of water began to fall. The three of them quickly changed into their waterproof clothing. The situation was looking bad.

"What's that?" asked Mark, pointing to some lights in the distance.

"It looks like the lights of a house," said Dad, peering into the darkness.

"I didn't see a house when we were here in the daylight," said Tim.

"I thought that there weren't any houses on the moor," said Mark.

"Well, it's there all right," said Dad, peering through the dark to try and get a better look. "Let's go and see if they'll help us."

They stumbled across the slippery heather as fast as they could and, ten minutes later, stood outside the front door of a large, brightly lit house.

Dad rang the bell. The door was

opened by a bald, jolly-looking man. He was about the same age as Dad.

"My goodness!" said the man, when he saw them. "Got stuck on the moor after dark, eh? You'd better come in." They took off their waterproofs in the hall and followed the man into his kitchen.

"Thanks ever so much," said Dad. "We've lost our map and compass and have been wandering around for hours."

"Easily done, easily done," insisted the man. "Come and get warm by the fire. Would you like something to eat?" They all shook their heads. No one was hungry. They were just very tired.

"We don't know what we'd have done if we hadn't seen your lights. I didn't think there were any houses on the moor," said Dad.

"This is the only one, but it's stood here for years," replied the man. He was going to talk more, but noticed how tired they all looked. "Here am I blabbering on, and you're nearly dropping on your feet," he said. "You must stay here tonight, and in the morning I'll point you in the right direction for the nearest village. It's about an hour's walk away."

"Would you mind if I used your phone to call my wife and let her know we're safe?" asked Dad.

"I'm terribly sorry," replied the man. "My phone's out of order. You can ring her when you reach the village in the morning."

He showed them upstairs to his spare bedroom and wished them a pleasant night's sleep.

There was one large double bed, which they all fell onto. They were too tired to even take their jackets off. They stretched out on the bed and moments later all three were fast asleep.

Halfway through the night, Mark awoke to a terrible smell of burning. Suddenly the bedroom door was flung wide open. The owner of the house stood there in his dressing gown, looking absolutely terrified.

"Wake up! Wake up!" he yelled. "The house is on fire! Get out, get out quickly…as fast as you can!"

"Dad! Tim! Wake up! The house is on fire!" cried Mark, shaking his father and brother awake. Dad sized up the situation at once. He quickly led the boys out into the hallway. There was so much smoke, they started to cough violently, and it was difficult to see. The heat was terrible and bright-orange flames licked at the walls and ceiling. Dad knew that they had to get out of the house as quickly as possible.

"Run, run!" he shouted at the boys, almost pushing them down the stairs. When they reached the bottom, they could just about see the front door through all the smoke. Dad yanked it open and they ran outside, taking in huge gulps of the fresh air.

When they were at a safe distance, they flopped down onto the moor, exhausted. Dad turned around, hoping to see that the owner of the house had got out safely too. He couldn't believe it. There was nothing there. No man, no burning house. Nothing except the empty moor. It was as if the house, its owner and the fire had never existed.

"Am I dreaming?" asked Dad in astonishment. "Where's the house gone, and the fire?"

"I…don't know, Dad," said Mark, his eyes wide with fear.

"This is really spooky," said Tim, almost in tears.

"I don't understand this. I don't understand this at all," whispered Dad, his eyes still searching for the burning house. Suddenly, he felt very afraid. "Run!" he yelled.

They ran over the heather, lit by the frantic beam of their torches, until they could run no more. Then they fell exhausted to the ground.

"We'll stay here and rest for a while," said Dad breathlessly. "It'll be light soon."

Dad couldn't sleep at all. While Mark and Tim dozed fitfully, everything that had happened that night went round and round in his head. At the first sign of daylight, he woke up the boys and told them that they should make a move. He didn't know which way to go, but had a strong feeling that if they followed the line of the rising sun, it would take them off the moor.

Two hours later Mark saw something gleaming in the distance.

"What's that?" he asked, screwing up his eyes to get a clearer look.

"I think it's a church spire!" Tim yelled.

They walked towards the spire as fast as their tired legs could carry them. As they got closer, they could make out houses too.

"We've done it!" Tim shouted.

"It must be the village that the man in the house was talking about," said Dad. They were so relieved to be safe again, they almost ran the last few yards. But the strain of their adventure started to show, and they felt exhausted and frozen as they walked into the village's main street.

A café was opening just across the road. They went inside and soon had their cold hands wrapped around mugs of hot tea. While Dad went to call Mum to tell her they were safe, the old man serving them shuffled over to their table with more tea.

"Excuse me," said Mark, looking up at him, "but is there a house on the moor?"

The old man scratched his head, thoughtfully.

"There *was* a house...owned by a friendly, jolly-looking man," he answered. "There was a fire in the house...burned the place down...his phone was out of order apparently...or he could have phoned for help. He had three guests that night...a man and his two sons. Luckily, he managed to get them out before the fire completely destroyed the house. He perished in the fire, unfortunately."

The boys couldn't believe what they were hearing.

"When was this?" asked Tim. "A week ago…a month…?"

"Oh no," laughed the old man. "I was not long out of school. It must have been…let me see …about 50 years ago."

The boys were so surprised, they gasped out loud and sent their tea crashing to the floor. When Dad came back to the table they told him exactly what the old man had said.

Although Mark, Tim and their dad recovered from the shock of what happened on the moor that night, not one of them ever went hiking on Ridlington Moor again. Funnily enough though, from that day on, Dad did believe in ghosts.

Amy
Makes
a Movie

Amy was upstairs in her bedroom reading her book. It was the summer holiday and all her friends were away. Amy was getting a little bored without her friends. She'd been to the library to choose some more books to read this morning, and she had already almost finished the first one. She was just starting the last chapter in her book when the phone rang. She heard her mother pick it up and then heard her shout, "It's for you, Amy. It's your godmother."

Amy ran downstairs, took the phone and, holding it very close to her ear, said, "Hello."

It was her godmother, Aunt Lavinia.

She was an actress and Amy sometimes saw her on TV. She could always tell when it was her because she spoke in a grand voice.

"Guess what," Aunt Lavinia said, getting right to the point as usual. "I've got a day's film-shooting this Sunday and I thought you might like to come along. It might be fun for you to see how they make films."

"Oh, I'd love to," Amy said, getting excited. She had seen Aunt Lavinia in a few movies and in quite a few commercials but she had no idea how they were actually made.

"That's marvellous," Aunt Lavinia said in that unmistakable voice. "I'll pick you up first thing in the morning. They like to start early."

That Sunday morning Amy woke up earlier than usual. She was just finishing her breakfast when she heard the toot! toot! of a car horn outside. Amy quickly got up from the table and put on her jacket. When the door opened, she couldn't believe her eyes. There was Aunt Lavinia in a bright red, open-top sports car.

Aunt Lavinia could see the look of surprise on the faces of Amy and her mother as they stared at the car.

"Do you like it?" she asked. "It belongs to my boyfriend, but he lets me borrow it from time to time." Then, sensing that Amy's mother might be concerned, she quickly added, "Don't worry, I won't break any speed limits."

Amy had never been in an open-top sports car before. It felt strange to have the wind blowing across her face. It was very exciting.

Aunt Lavinia's hair flew wildly about in the wind. But she was a very good driver.

Most of the time she kept her eyes fixed on the road, though now and then she turned to say something, but the wind would whoosh the words away. So all Amy heard was something like "w h a a a - a a a - y y y y - y y y y y - a a l l l l l - l l l l l l l - w w w w - w w i i i - i i g g g g g - g g g h t?" She guessed she was being asked if she was all right, but she knew there was no point in answering because her words would be whooshed away as well. So she just nodded.

When they arrived at the studio, Aunt Lavinia said, "Now, you stay close to me because it's a big place. It can be very confusing and, if you don't know your way around, it's easy to get lost."

Amy did as she was told although she found it hard to keep up with Aunt Lavinia because she walked so quickly.

The film studios were huge – like a village. There were lots of different buildings with numbers on the side. Aunt Lavinia had a piece of paper that told them which building to report to.

After walking for about ten minutes, they found the right building. Aunt Lavinia showed her piece of paper to a man dressed like a security guard and he pointed to some double doors on the left. They found themselves in a long corridor and walked past a number of doors with titles on them. When they reached a door that had MAKE-UP written on the outside, Aunt Lavinia opened it. Inside there were a few people sitting in chairs being made up.

One of the make-up artists recognized her.

"Lavinia!"she called out. "You'd better take a seat, I think you'll be called very soon."

"I guess I'd better get ready," Aunt Lavinia said. Amy watched with interest as the make-up artist worked on Aunt Lavinia's face. But, when the hairdresser arrived, Amy began to feel fidgety.

"I'm afraid this is going to take ages, Amy. Would you like to get yourself a drink and a snack at the canteen?"

Aunt Lavinia called over to a friend who was standing nearby. "Nigel, would you be a dear and take my goddaughter, Amy, to the canteen so she can get a snack?" Nigel agreed. Aunt Lavinia took out three pound coins.

"Here you are, Amy," she said. "I think you'll find the canteen fun but, when you finish, be sure to come back here and we'll walk to the set together."

Amy found the canteen a very curious place. She had never seen anything like it. The room itself looked like any other canteen. What made it so unusual was the people who were there. Sitting at one table was Frankenstein's monster eating a chocolate doughnut. And next to him was Dracula tucking into a bacon roll. The whole room seemed to be filled with strange characters from stories. Nigel could see that Amy was startled.

"Oh, don't mind them," he said. "They're all actors taking a break." To show her what he meant, he turned to Frankenstein's monster, gave him a thumbs up, and said, "All right, Dave?" Frankenstein's monster looked over, smiled and gave a little wave.

Nigel then asked Amy what she wanted to eat. She told him and handed over her coins. Then he said, "Go and find yourself a seat. I'll bring the food over."

The only empty seat that Amy could see was next to a knight, dressed in armour, who was trying to eat a piece of apple pie. But every time he took a bite, his metal beak fell on his fork with a loud clang.

"Come and take a bite with us!" Dracula called to Amy, pulling out a seat next to him. Amy sat down and hoped that Nigel would be quick getting the food. She smiled nervously at Frankenstein's monster as she watched Dracula squirt tomato sauce on his bacon roll. Nigel brought Amy a hamburger and coke, which she ate rather more quickly than usual. As soon as she'd finished, she said goodbye and went to find her godmother.

When Amy finally found the make-up room it was empty. She looked around and saw that there was a door at the far side of the room. She guessed Aunt Lavinia must have gone through there after they'd finished her make-up and hair. Amy opened the door and found herself in a dark, narrow passage. It felt a little creepy and for a second she wanted to turn back, but she told herself not to be silly and kept going.

She was walking very slowly now, feeling her way along by holding onto the wall. Once or twice she stumbled because she couldn't really see where she was going. Finally she saw a glimmer of light. This made her feel better and she began to walk faster. She noticed that the floor was becoming wider as the lights got brighter.

She could hear a man's voice shouting: "CUT! This scene just isn't working. It needs a link."

Suddenly she felt a blaze of hot lights shining right on her face. They were so hot and blinding that she had to cover her eyes. At the same time she heard the man's voice again:

"Who is that?" he asked. "Is that girl in the script?"

Then she heard Aunt Lavinia's voice. "AMY! How did you get here?"

She was on some sort of stage set and there were a lot of people busily moving about around her. But she couldn't really see because the lights were so dazzling. Amy felt confused and frightened.

A woman's voice shouted, "GET THE GIRL OFF THE SET!" And she saw someone walking quickly towards her.

Then the man's voice broke in again.

"WAIT!" it said, very dramatically. Amy's eyes were getting used to the bright lights and she could now see a little more clearly. She saw that the voice belonged to the director, who was sitting in front of the stage in a special chair. It was obvious that he was in charge of what was going on. He stood up, walked to the camera and took a long look through the lens.

"Yes," he said, almost to himself… "that's very interesting…this could be just what we need."

The woman who had been sent to remove Amy was now standing almost next to her. She turned to the director.

"Do you want her in or out?" she asked.

"In," the director replied.

Amy still didn't understand what was going on. Aunt Lavinia hurried towards her.

"Congratulations, Amy!" she said excitedly. "You're going to be in the movie!"

Amy couldn't believe it. She was actually going to be in a film. She was so surprised that she almost didn't hear the director, who was talking to her again.

"What's your name?" he asked.

"Amy," she replied softly. "Amy Dobson."

"Now, Amy," he said, "if you're going to be in this film, it might be better if you said something. Do you think you could handle that?"

Amy suddenly felt nervous. She would

have to say something in front of all these people, under the spotlight with the camera pointing at her. So when she answered she could barely whisper.

"I'm sorry, I couldn't hear you," the director said, in a surprisingly friendly voice. "Could you repeat that?"

"Yes, I think so," Amy answered in a strained voice that she didn't recognize as her own. "It depends how much I've got to say."

"Oh, it won't be very much," he said reassuringly. "Perhaps a line or two."

"Will I get paid?" she asked.

It must have been a funny question because everybody suddenly started laughing. She didn't know why she had asked that question. Somehow it had just popped out. Now she was blushing bright red, but in a funny sort of way it took away her nervousness, and she joined in with the laughter. The director was laughing too.

"Of course you'll get paid," he said. "Gloria, my assistant, will draw up a contract and then you and your mother can sign it. Now Amy," he continued, "I'm going to give you a couple of lines. I want you to walk up to Lavinia and say, 'That's a nice dress, did you just buy it?' Do you think you could handle that?"

"I think so," Amy said, but she didn't sound very confident.

"Good," the director said. "I'll get Gloria to write out the line for you. She'll print it nice and big so it'll be easy to read. Then you can practise it a few times until you're completely comfortable with it. Once you feel you've got it, we'll give you a bit of make-up, and then we'll get the cameras rolling. Does that sound all right?"

Amy nodded and walked off the stage. She found a wall against which there were a few empty chairs and sat in one of them. It was the first chance she'd had to relax.

A few minutes later an attractive girl, who Amy guessed must be Gloria, came over and handed her a sheet of paper. On the sheet was written the line she'd heard before. She looked at it for several minutes. Then she practised saying the line over and over again until she knew it by heart. Once she knew it, she folded the sheet of paper and put it in her pocket. Then she began practising the line again, but this time by putting the emphasis on different words.

Once it came out as, "*That's* a nice dress, did you just buy it? which sounded natural. But when she tried, "That's a nice dress, did *you* just buy it?" it sounded strange. After trying out almost every combination, Amy decided to put the main stress on 'That's'.

She had been practising for about ten

minutes when the director came over and told her not to overdo it because "you'll just drive yourself crazy". Then he sent her to the make-up room, where the same woman who had been working on Aunt Lavinia began working on her. This made her feel very important. When she was finished, Amy looked in the mirror and was surprised to see how bright the make-up looked. The woman smiled. "It looks over the top in here," she said. "But when the camera picks it up, it will seem natural."

When she got back, everyone seemed to be taking a break. Amy quickly spotted Aunt Lavinia. As usual, she was surrounded by people who were laughing at one of her stories. That was one of the things Amy loved about her godmother – she could tell a great story.

No sooner had Aunt Lavinia introduced Amy to her friends, than the director shouted, "Quiet please, places everyone! We're going to roll in a minute."

Everything went quiet for a second, and then suddenly there was a lot of rushing around as everyone got into their positions. The cameramen raced to their cameras, the technicians went about their business and the actors who were 'on' headed for the stage. Aunt Lavinia took the stairs on the right and Amy headed for the opposite side.

"All right," the director said, once everybody was in place. "Now Amy, listen carefully because this is for real. When I yell 'Action' I want you to walk towards

Lavinia and start saying your line when you're about four feet away. Got that?"

Amy hunched her shoulders. It was her way of preparing herself. But she didn't know she was doing it. She felt a little as if she were getting ready for a race on Sports Day.

"Here we go," the director shouted. "LIGHTS."

The lights, which had been toned down, flashed on at full power.

"CAMERAS."

The cameras started to whirr.

"ACTION!"

The whole room suddenly became completely silent except for the cameras. Amy started walking. One step, then another. Aunt Lavinia seemed so far away. She would have to walk for a mile before she reached her. She heard her shoes squeak and wondered if anybody else heard them. Just keep going, she told herself.

She was getting closer now, much closer. One more step and it would be time to speak. "That's a nice dress," she began, "did you just…" She couldn't remember the rest of the words. "Did you just…"

"CUT!" the director yelled.

The cameras suddenly stopped. "That's all right, Amy," he said, reassuringly. "Don't get upset. It happens to the best of them. Even Mary Kate and Ashley sometimes forget their lines. Let's try it again." Then he raised his voice. "Back to your original positions, everyone."

Amy raced back to the other side of the stage. She was surprised to find that this time the stage didn't seem as large as it did before.

"Stand by," the director shouted. "Here we go. Cameras and…ACTION!"

This time Amy felt more comfortable.

She was much more relaxed as she walked. It was funny how much of a difference a little experience can make. She was now approaching Aunt Lavinia.

"That's a nice dress," she said, sounding quite confident. "Did *you* just buy it?"

As soon as she said the words she knew that they sounded wrong. She clenched her right hand into a fist and kicked out with her right foot even before she heard the dreaded word that she knew was coming up…

"CUT!"

The director stood up and walked over to Amy. He put his arm around her to calm her down and said, "Now Amy, the worst thing you can do is get cross with yourself. Any actor will tell you that. That just throws your timing and everything else right off. Now we're going to do it again, so get ready to have another go. But, before you do, I want you to clear your mind, relax and…" He now lowered his voice, "…and just think in a calm way about your words, about your line. And you'll find it will come very naturally. Have you got that?"

Amy nodded.

"Good," he said and he walked back to his chair. Once he sat down, he didn't hesitate.

"All right, everybody. Here we go. ACTION!"

As soon as Amy heard the word, she was in her stride. Very calmly, just as he instructed her, she started to walk and she did just as he said. She concentrated on her line. Not by gripping it as tightly as she could in her mind, but by keeping it loose and relaxed.

Before she knew it, she was in front of Aunt Lavinia. She looked up at her godmother's smiling face. This time there was nothing to worry about.

"*That's* a nice dress," she said. "Did you just buy it?" She said it as if it were the most natural thing in the world. As if she were saying it to Aunt Lavinia in her sitting room at home.

"Why no, my dear," Aunt Lavinia replied, and Amy could see that she was proud of her. "I've had this for years. That's what happens when you buy quality."

"CUT!" the director yelled. "That's it." Then he added, "Well done, everybody, that's a wrap."

All the cameramen cheered. Aunt Lavinia rushed over to give Amy a big hug.

A few of the technicians even broke into applause.

Then the director came over and he gave Amy a hug as well. "That third reading was absolutely perfect," he said. "Are you sure you haven't done this before?"

Amy was about to say "no" but he beat her to it.

"How does it feel to be an actress?" he asked.

Amy didn't even have to think. She took a quick look at Aunt Lavinia, then at the director, and then gave her answer.

"Great," she said.